BETWEEN

Books by Jean Thesman

Between

A Sea So Far

In the House of the Queen's Beasts

Calling the Swan

The Other Ones

The Tree of Bells

The Moonstones

The Storyteller's Daughter

The Ornament Tree

Summerspell

Cattail Moon

Nothing Grows Here

Molly Donnelly

When the Road Ends

The Rain Catchers

Appointment with a Stranger

Rachel Chance

The Last April Dancers

BETWEEN

JEAN THESMAN

VIKING

VIKING

Published by the Penguin Group
Penguin Putnam Books for Young Readers,
345 Hudson Street, New York, New York 10014, U.S.A.
Penguin Books Ltd, 80 Strand, London WC2R 0RL, England
Penguin Books Australia Ltd, Ringwood, Victoria, Australia
Penguin Books Canada Ltd, 10 Alcorn Avenue, Toronto, Ontario, Canada M4V 3B2
Penguin Books (N.Z.) Ltd, 182-190 Wairau Road, Auckland 10, New Zealand

Penguin Books Ltd, Registered Offices: Harmondsworth, Middlesex, England

10 9 8 7 6 5 4 3 2 1

LIBRARY OF CONGRESS CATALOGING-IN-PUBLICATION DATA
Thesman, Jean.
Between / by Jean Thesman.
p. cm.
Summary: Sent to stay at guest house near Puget Sound   , Charlotte
finds herself worried that she is losing her mind because o   ge goings-on
involving her adopted younger brother, a talking cat, a mena   couple of
guests, and the mysterious woods nearby.
ISBN 0-670-03561-0
[1. Fairy tales. 2. Brothers and sisters—Fiction.] I. Title
PZ8.T355 Be 2002
[Fic]—dc21 2001046908

Printed in U.S.A.
Set in Bookman
Design by Nancy Brennan

 *For Cassie*

Introduction

Charlotte Thacker, a pioneer environmentalist and nature photographer, left a box of papers for safekeeping with her niece, Elizabeth Prescott, before she began her last journey in 1980. The box contained, among other things, the notebook Charlotte kept during the summer of 1941, when she was fourteen, and a folder of observations of a place called Darkwood. The author of these observations is unknown.

Curiously, the box contained no photographs.

Chapter 1

June 1941

An old car passed Darkwood late in a humid June afternoon, and the moment it was out of sight, a cloud of small, glimmering creatures rose from the tall grass beside the road and streamed deep into the woods. Their alarm cries were unintelligible to most of the inhabitants of the forest, a source of irritation to them rather than a warning. Only the Fox Fairy paid attention, and when they vanished among the trees, he stared after them, head cocked to one side, while he considered the possibilities.

Finally he trotted to the edge of a clearing and sat before an ancient hollow tree. "Midwife, the Spirit Lights say that they saw someone passing by in the road, someone important. They said 'Prince.' I heard the word distinctly."

The Old Midwife Tree awoke from her nap, furious. She thrashed her branches and showered the Fox Fairy with twigs and leaves, then shouted, "Spirit Lights? They say? Nobody knows what they say—and nobody cares. Mindless nitwits! You woke me up for this?" She scattered another storm of twigs and half of an abandoned bird's nest on the Fox Fairy, who calmly rose to shake himself off and then sat down again to wait out her tantrum.

The Old Midwife Tree was ancient, but she was not a tree. She had taken that form after the Invasion of the Mudwalkers, sulking at the edge of the clearing and complaining endlessly. Everyone always listened respectfully, although most of her troubles were the same as their own. She was the only Elder who had survived the Invasion. She was wise, but her memories of the old times in Darkwood were fading, it seemed, and this frightened the others more than her occasional rages. Anchored as she was to the earth by the roots she herself had created, there was little she could do to them if they kept out of reach of her thrashing branches and wildly flung twigs. But if she lost her memories of their history, then they were all in danger.

"The Spirit Lights say that our Prince might have come," the Fox Fairy said.

The Midwife Tree was silent for a moment. Then she cried, "You're an idiot! We have waited in vain. It has all been in vain."

There was no calming her now, so the Fox Fairy stretched out and rested his chin on his neat paws.

A Unicorn hurried into the clearing. "Midwife, here is someone to visit you," she said soothingly, pushing her colt toward the Midwife. The colt dug in her heels stubbornly at first, and then she impudently butted at the old tree with her tiny new horn.

Her mother pulled her back by her mane, perhaps yanking a little harder than was necessary. The colt squeaked and ran off, her small hoofs clicking on stones. She disappeared into the wood, and moments later, a flock of Sky Wing Spirits suddenly burst into shrieks.

"It's all in vain and nobody in his right mind would believe a word the Spirit Lights say!" the Midwife cried again, thrashing branches and moaning.

"Everything will be all right," the Unicorn said. She rubbed her face against Midwife's trunk, hoping to calm her. "Remember, we were promised that the Prince would return to us."

"Oh, do shut up!" the Midwife snapped. "Go catch your brat before she betrays all of us. She'll be running down the road next, blatting her silly head off."

The Unicorn sighed and moved off. She heard, in the distance, Walking Wing Spirits taking clumsy flight, clacking wildly. "Daughter! Stop that!" she called, but her daughter did not answer.

The Fox Fairy said, "She told you true, Midwife. We were promised." A few of the Spirit Lights had returned, and they clustered about him anxiously.

5

"Idiot!" the Midwife yelled. "Go away!" She showered him with twigs, and the alarmed Spirit Lights flew off in an agitated, glimmering ball, twittering to one another in a language that no one completely understood.

The Fox Fairy shook his head and left. The Midwife suspected that he was laughing at her.

"Idiot!" she called after him. He did not turn back, but changed into a dark weasel and disappeared into a hole beneath a salmonberry bush. He, more than most of them, still had the strength to shape-shift at will. "Oh, it isn't fair!" the Midwife wept bitterly. "We waited for nothing."

"Quiet!" rumbled the young Dragon in his egg, deep in the mud at the bottom of the pond. "Quiet up there!"

The Midwife, exhausted by her tantrum, fell into an abrupt sleep, and the wood was quiet again. Summer days passed as if nothing had happened. Only the Fox Fairy and the Spirit Lights remained watchful.

FROM CHARLOTTE THACKER'S NOTEBOOK

I was changing bed sheets in the big unpainted room I shared with my older sister and younger brother in the attic of Gull Walk, and I straightened up when I heard them in the yard below me. They were lucky, being sent to work in the vegetable garden instead of the hot guest house attic on a sunny afternoon. I leaned out the open window to call to them—and my world changed abruptly.

Meg and Will were walking past the laundry drying on a line sagging between the back porch and the gate that opened to the garden. The late afternoon sun cast Meg's shadow on a crisp white sheet hanging still in the windless afternoon. And the sun also cast the shadow of the rake Will carried over his bony shoulder. But Will's shadow was not there.

Impossible.

I, Charlotte Thacker, might have just finished eighth grade, but I knew that any object between the sun and a big white sheet would cast a shadow on that sheet. Yet only Meg's shadow—and the rake's—moved down the path to the gate. Will followed Meg, bouncing a little the way he always did, his overalls too long for a twelve-year-old boy and wrinkling around his ankles, his old black sneakers puffing up dust. The rake's shadow bounced. The unpainted wooden gate opened and shut, and then Meg and Will were out of sight.

I could feel the slick, painted windowsill under my hands and smell the faint scent of the sweet peas that grew against the lattice wall of the porch, so I knew I was not dreaming. But my ears were ringing from shock. What I had seen could not have happened.

I moved to the bed and sat down suddenly. My sharp headache was surely the fault of the heat and the dusty smells in the attic—the two rooms under the peaked roof of the guesthouse had not been used for many years, not since live-in servants had been there. But what if I was sick? If I had caught Mama's tuberculosis after all, then I, too, would be sent to a sanatorium and be unable to have visitors or even write letters. What more could happen to the Thacker family?

But wait, wait, I told myself sternly. I wasn't coughing, and, except for the headache—and a little dizziness—I felt fine. Will had a shadow—of course he did!—and I, practical Charlotte, was being ridiculous.

It's just staying in a strange place and not knowing what's happening to Mama, I thought. Worried people probably imagine all sorts of nonsense.

But I had noticed other strange things since we had come here to Gull Walk to stay with the Warders—things about Will. I had considered talking to Meg, but at fifteen, she was still a tattletale, and she would write to Dad immediately, accusing me of picking on Will—or inventing things—or perhaps even outright lying. But something had gone wrong after we moved to Gull Walk. It was wrong with Will—and maybe even with me.

No, it's my imagination, I thought. I pushed my short brown hair back from my forehead and took off my glasses, polishing them on the loose shirt that was a hand-me-down from Meg. It's all *nothing*, I thought. In a while, my brother and sister will come back from the garden and I'll see both of their shadows on the sheets, and I'll know that my mind was playing tricks

on me. I was nervous because Mama was sick and Dad
had been recalled by the Navy and sent off to Hawaii,
and the three of us had been shifted from one place to
another like unwanted puppies. It was hard not to feel
resentful, too. First we'd gone to Aunt and Uncle Tate,
but Aunt Milly had had her new baby a month too
early and couldn't take care of us as well as her own,
so there we were, with Helen and Scotty Tate, in a run-
down, nearly empty old guesthouse at the beach with
strangers.

No wonder I thought my brother didn't have a shadow.
And had learned to talk to birds.

Cousin Helen Tate, who was a few months older
than Meg, shared a small room across the hall with
six-year-old Scotty, and the two of them had gone to
town with Mr. Warder in his old car, so I was expected
to change their sheets, too. According to Uncle Ned,
everybody had to help out at the guesthouse because
the Warders were getting very little money to keep five
children for the entire summer. Times were hard, and
Uncle Ned, desperate, had laid claim to a very distant
kinship with Mr. Warder, and that good man had come
through with an invitation for the summer.

Gull Walk had only two paying guests at the
moment, an elderly, unpleasant couple, the Fletchers,
who had been coming twice a year for eight years.
Aside from them, there had been only three people who

had stayed there recently, drop-ins on their way around Puget Sound.

"First it was the Depression and now it's all the war talk," Miss Warder had explained to us after we arrived. "People aren't in the mood for vacations in out-of-the-way places when nobody knows what's going to happen next. Calling back the servicemen like your poor father wasn't a good sign."

Mr. Warder shrugged and said, "There's no reason for any of us to worry. Those rumors won't come to much. Anyway, not many people want to stay in this old place when there are those fancy new motels down the road on the other side of town." The old man had seemed oddly pleased at what might have been considered a disaster by someone else, and he had ruffled Will's silvery hair with his broad hand while he laughed. "But we'll get by. Gull Walk—and the Warders—have been here for a long time, and we'll be here a long time from now."

But just in case of a sudden flood of unexpected guests, his sister had put us in the two attic rooms. "Summer has hardly begun," she said. "Who knows what might happen?" Behind her back, her brother had shaken his head and winked at me.

I had a new worry to add to the many that kept me awake so long every night. What if the Warders had to close Gull Walk because there were no paying guests to keep it open? Where would we end up next? My life had seemed to be a string of nightmares, ugly beads strung together on the dark thread of Mama's illness, like a necklace made by a cruel troll. After Mama had been taken away in an ambulance, Dad had cared for us until the Navy had called him back—temporarily, he had said—to the base in Hawaii. We had moved in with the Tates in Seattle—until the rainy afternoon when all of us children, Thackers and Tates alike, were unceremoniously stuffed into an old bus at the depot by frantic Uncle Ned and sent off on a journey that had taken most of the day.

We, the Thackers, had never been to Gull Walk and had never met the Warders, but our cousins, who had vacationed with their parents at the beach twice before, assured us that they knew exactly where to get off the bus.

"Don't worry," chubby Helen had added with her own special brand of sniffy superiority that was aggravating me more than I dared admit to myself. "The Warders *always* meet the bus when they know people are coming. Someone will pick us up at the depot."

But I hadn't been reassured, although Meg had only shrugged. My pretty sister was wrapped in her own personal misery because her boyfriend, Angus, never particularly faithful to her anyway, probably would find another girl before the summer was over.

Will had seemed anxious on the bus, too, so I slipped my arm over his thin shoulder. He was so small for his age, so thin. His silvery blond hair and large

dark eyes only accentuated his look of frailty. Meg and I were both robust girls with bright blue eyes, and next to us, Will always appeared to be fragile. But, as Mama had once said, who knew where he had been or what had happened to him in the first few years of his life? Will had been four when my family adopted him from an orphanage connected with our church.

And now he had lost his parents again.

But cheerful, rumpled Mr. Warder had met us at the small bus depot in town after all, and I was reassured by his big smile and vigorous handshake. Maybe things would be all right, I had thought. Maybe.

However, there had been that small, disturbing incident when we arrived at Gull Walk. Mr. Warder's sister had met us on the front porch and greeted us kindly. But later, after showing us upstairs to the attic rooms, she had looked at Will for a long time and then said in a strained voice, "My, you don't look much like your sisters, do you?"

I had heard that comparison over and over, ever since my parents adopted Will, but before I could give my standard (and untrue) answer—"Maybe he looks like our great-grandmother"—Helen blabbed, "He was adopted when he was little, so he doesn't look like anybody."

I had always felt that this information was no one's business, especially since it brought on too many questions, and so I felt betrayed by Helen, who could be counted on to offer strangers any sort of gossip that could make a person uncomfortable. Meg and I rewarded her with ferocious scowls, which she ignored. Will merely had shrugged and scuffed the toe of his sneaker on the threadbare carpet.

"Adopted," repeated Miss Warder, and she looked at Will for so long that finally he blushed. "Adopted," she said again, weakly, as if she had never heard the word before. And then, seeing my outraged expression, she said, "How lucky you girls are to have such a fine brother."

But she had nearly choked on the words, and I had not forgiven her for a couple of days. Meg had advised me to forget the matter—hadn't we heard it all before dozens of times and didn't some people have peculiar opinions about adoption?—but I watched Miss Warder carefully to make sure that she did not ask Will any of the usual questions: "Where did you come from?" "Do you remember your real parents?" "What happened to them?"

Or worst of all, "Are you illegitimate?" As if that was anyone's business.

But Miss Warder said nothing more, which was just as well. The adoption agency had said that Will's background was unknown, and Mama and Dad had said that it did not matter anyway, since he was exactly the sort of boy the family needed and wanted.

The difficult time with Miss Warder passed, and even though we still did not feel at home at Gull Walk, we had become comfortable enough to find ways to entertain ourselves, and even argue with each other the way we had all of our lives.

I finished making up the double bed and Will's narrow cot, and then crossed the hall to make my cousins' beds. The two boys should have been sharing this small room, but after we arrived, Will began having screaming nightmares, and he disturbed Scotty too much. Helen's clothes hung from hooks on the wall, but Scotty's were still in the box his father had packed. I thought about putting them away in the small chest of drawers and decided against it. Scotty would not mind, but Helen could be sharp-tongued. She might think that I was snooping. The awful truth was that the only snoop among us was Helen herself.

When I returned to the window in my own room, I saw that Miss Warder was taking down the last dry sheet and folding it before putting it in the wicker clothes basket, and I sighed with relief. The whole silly shadow thing had existed only in my imagination, and with the last of the sheets gone from the line, there was no chance of my dreaming up something that stupid again. I would be able to laugh about it one day, when we were all back in our own house again and safe forever.

But as I watched, the back gate opened and Will and Meg walked through. Meg's long shadow moved along the grass in the drying yard.

Will's shadow hurried to catch up to him, dancing a little, waving its hands, eager not to be left behind. Will did not seem to notice. His attention was fixed on a brown sparrow balancing on the clothesline, and his lips were moving. The sparrow fluttered to his shoulder for a moment and then flew away.

I shut my eyes tight and pressed my hands against my mouth. This was no time to go crazy or get sick or have trouble with my eyes. All the family had had complete physicals, and we were all fine, except Mama. At least so far. We would need more tests at regular intervals, the doctors had explained. But was this—this delusion!—an early sign of illness?

I shook my head. Mama had never acted crazy or seen things that did not exist. She had just grown thinner and thinner, and finally she could not stop coughing, so the doctors had sent her away.

I took one last look out the window and saw Jonah, the teenage boy the Warders had taken in after his parents died. Thin and shaggy and brownish-blond, he looked up at the window as he walked under it, saw me, and did not smile. He was tossing a screwdriver idly from hand to hand, never missing. Supposedly he did chores around the hotel, too, but I had never seen him do anything at all. More often than not, I had caught him napping on the porch or in the hammock or in the doorway of the collapsing boathouse near the cliff. He went barefoot, inside and out, and wore the same ragged, faded overalls every day.

I turned away. I was not sure how I felt about Jonah, but he was not around much except for meals. Apparently he spent his nights in the boathouse or on the porch swing. Meg had said that he gave her a creepy feeling when he looked at her, as if he could read her mind. But boy-crazy Helen had flirted a little with him—until he sneered at her, and after that she could not say enough bad things about him, his clothes, his mussy hair, and those bare feet.

But I had a secret reason for disliking Jonah. He talked to Will too much. He went out of his way to get my brother alone. On their fourth evening at Gull Walk, I had walked into one of their conversations, this time in the side yard where an old wooden picnic table sat under a peach tree. Jonah had been saying, ". . . and everyone was weak after the long winter, and so many trees had been cut down, and no one knew they were coming until it was too late, and nearly everyone died in the battle . . ." He had seen me then, scowled furiously, and walked away.

"What were you talking about?" I had asked Will.

Will smiled innocently. "Birds," he had said.

He had never lied to me before.

Chapter 2

"I have come from the guardians' house," the Fox Fairy said as he sat beneath the Old Midwife Tree and curled his tail neatly around his front feet.

"So what?" the Midwife said angrily. She shook her branches and an elderly Tree Spirit, in the form of a squirrel, fell awkwardly to the ground. It stood up, shook itself off, and limped away toward a wild cherry tree where half a dozen Sky Wing Spirits practiced for a concert. The Sky Wings stopped singing and flew down to cluster around the squirrel, who had much to say about the Old Midwife Tree and her foul temper.

"Why should I care about the guardians?" the Midwife asked the Fox Fairy. "What have they ever done for me?"

"Who could do anything for you after you grew roots?" the Fox Fairy asked. He was becoming testy. "You sit in the same place and then complain about the view! You were better company when you were a—"

The Midwife deliberately snapped off a branch and

flung it at him. "I am better company than you deserve. Are you going to tell me about the guardians or are you going to sit there and argue?"

The Fox Fairy sighed. "I have studied the young Mudwalkers at the house," he said. "One of them is the right age to be the Prince, and his shadow will go with me whenever I call it."

The Midwife stood very still, so still that she almost looked like a real tree. "Are you sure?" she asked. "Are you sure you didn't imagine it?"

The Fox Fairy growled, insulted. "Of course I'm sure. I called his shadow several times, and it always turned and ran to me. It remembers me, even if he does not."

"If you're lying, I swear and promise and declare that I will fall on you and crush you to ratty fur and skinny bones . . ."

The Fox Fairy's eyes lighted gold for an instant, and he sprang up into a great, tusked beast that grabbed the Midwife Tree in its jaws and shook it. The Midwife Tree let out a squawk, and the great beast let go and dropped back into his fox shape.

"Make no threats," he said quietly. "Make no threats to me. You may know all of our history, but I know enough to save us."

From deep below the pond, the Dragon said, "Quiet! Or I will rise up now and settle all quarrels and answer all questions—and you do not want that to happen."

The Fox Fairy flicked his tail and ran off to harass the

squirrel for a few entertaining minutes. The Old Midwife Tree tossed her branches irritably, swatted at a Spirit Light that had lost its way to a meeting on the other side of the clearing, and settled down for a long sulk. She fell asleep before she could complete it, something that often happened.

From Charlotte Thacker's notebook

As I went down the bare back stairs to the kitchen, I passed the door to the second floor where there were seven empty rooms made up for guests who might or might not come. My footsteps had echoed on the polished boards, giving me the feeling that someone—or something—was behind me, watching me. But the old place did not seem haunted, just deeply saddened because it had been nearly abandoned. Or so I thought. I had caught myself brooding and imagining more since we moved into Gull Walk.

The newer hotels farther down the road past the woods were much more appealing. There even were two modern auto courts with lighted "vacancy" signs that flashed on and off. Perhaps, with fresh paint and new carpets, Gull Walk might attract vacationers again, when there was no more talk of the United States entering the war in Europe or being attacked by Japan, and people felt free to spend money. Certainly

19

I would feel more secure if the place were full, because Meg, Helen, and I would be needed as maids and waitresses. Security came from filling a need.

Miss Warder was baking lemon pies in the kitchen, and the whole lower floor smelled wonderfully sweet and sour, both at the same time. My mouth watered as I pushed open the swinging door and asked if I could help.

Miss Warder, thin and gray as a dry stick, looked up from beating egg whites for the meringue and said, "If you wouldn't mind, would you pick some of the sweet peas and put them in the vase on the Fletchers' table in the dining room? I like things to be pretty for the guests."

"Ferns look nice with flowers. Should I pick some of them, too?" I asked, anxious to help out, anxious to make myself indispensable, even though we had only been there a week. People who are indispensable will always have a place to stay, I reasoned, even though that plan had not worked out with my aunt and uncle. I *could* have helped with the baby when he came home from the hospital after he was strong enough! I protested to myself. I could have done *all* of the laundry . . .

Perhaps Meg had been right. Our aunt and uncle did not want us around the new baby, just in case we were infected with TB, too. Just in case it showed up in us later on. It could happen, Meg had said. We were lucky that our friends had not abandoned us.

Miss Warder liked the idea of ferns and handed me

a pair of scissors. I hurried out, passing my brother and sister in the back hall. "Be sure to wash," I warned Will. Miss Warder became concerned about him when he was grubby, for fear that he might get sick, and sometimes Will could be surprisingly rebellious, not at all the way he had been at home.

"I will, I will!" he protested. His face was dirty, too. Even his elbows!

"I already told him," Meg said, sighing. "He ought to take a bath."

"No!" Will ran ahead of me and took the stairs two at a time. "No bath now. Later. Maybe."

I let the screen door slam behind me. Oh, Will, I thought. What was I thinking? You're just an ordinary boy, grubby and needing a haircut, not a child without a shadow. Or with a shadow that runs after him, waving its hands, as if it wanted him to stop and wait.

Half the sweet peas stubbornly bore only tightly wrapped buds, but I found several half-blown pink flowers near the bottom of the lattice on the west side of the porch. I cut the stems carefully on a slant and then chose two fronds of delicate maidenhair ferns. Mama would have liked the combination. Thinking of her caused a lump to form in my throat.

Dad had made us promise to write to Mama once a week, even though she could not answer the letters because of the possibility of contagion. And we were to write to him once a week, too, faithfully. He would answer just as faithfully, he had said. So far we had written six times to Mama and twice to Dad. But did Dad even know where we were yet? Uncle Ned had said he would contact him right away. It took forever for a letter to get to Hawaii.

Nobody knows where we are, I thought, miserable and close to tears. You can't get more lost than that.

I bent down to clip off a particularly nice blossom and saw a yellow cat staring at me through the lattice under the porch. I froze, surprised. The Warders had no pets, and I had not seen the cat before.

The cat, his back arched, watched me intently with glowing golden eyes—and his expression turned to disdain and a rather offensive kind of pity. Then he sat and licked a front paw, elaborately ignoring me. Obviously the interview was over.

I stepped back, irritated for a moment. But then, feeling sorry for the creature whose washing had not made the paw cleaner, I bent down and said, "Hey, kitty, are you lost?"

"Are *you* lost?" the cat asked distinctly.

I blinked, but the cat did not. *"What?"* I blurted, clutching the flowers to my chest.

The cat turned away, apparently disgusted with my company and general ignorance, and he disappeared far back into the shadows under the porch.

I wasn't dreaming. This had really happened. *Hadn't it?*

The screen door banged, startling me, and Meg came outside, carrying a glass of lemonade. Had she seen or heard anything?

"There's a glass for you on the kitchen table, if you're done with the flowers," she said as she sat on the swing. "You look hot, Charlotte. Are you feeling all right?"

"I'm fine," I said quickly. "Are you the one who made the lemonade?"

"Just the way Mama does," Meg said, sipping from her glass.

Both my hands were full, so Meg opened the screen door for me. "Don't worry so much," Meg told me, suddenly kinder than usual. "Mama will get better and we'll be home by the time Dad comes back. Everything will be all right."

"I know," I said, not daring to believe. How confident would my sister be of anything if she had heard a talking cat?

"You all right, dear?" Miss Warder asked when she saw me coming into the kitchen.

I, still thinking of the cat and my brother's shadow, said, "I'm fine, thank you." I was certain I sounded normal enough, so lying must come easier with practice, I decided. I should have felt ashamed for thinking such a thing, but I didn't. If I had died at that moment, no doubt I would have gone straight to hell—but I certainly had a good excuse.

"Why don't you go down to the beach for a while when

23

you're finished with the flowers?" Miss Warder said as she ran water over crisp lettuce at the sink. "Inhale that good salt air. That will keep you healthy. I'll send somebody out for you when it's time for dinner."

I arranged the flowers in the vase in the dining room, then took my lemonade outside gladly. I told Meg that I was going to the beach, adding an unenthusiastic invitation to come along, and I was not sorry when she turned me down in favor of staying on the porch. She was reading a movie magazine and barely looked up when I spoke to her.

Skin prickling, I hurried past the place where my brother first had no shadow and then had one hastily running after him. It was just an ordinary day and I was an ordinary girl. There was nothing here that I needed to worry about. I walked through the weather-beaten gate, along the path beside the vegetable garden, and down the narrow road that led to the collapsing boathouse. The road was not much more than a soft dirt path, and I noticed the footprints of a horse crossing it in one place, and farther along, I saw the smaller tracks of a dog. I stopped to look around, but the animals that had left their marks were gone.

The road ended a few feet from the boathouse. Storms and tides had washed away the coarse sand and rocks until the boathouse teetered on an edge of low cliff beyond the reach of the water. There was no boat now, no dock. A ragged line of rotting pilings staggered out on the wet gray sand and gravel that stretched to the ebbing tide. I saw that Gull Walk was located at the end of a slender finger of Puget Sound, isolated from everything. Across the water, the forest had been logged off, and young alders and maples covered most of the ravaged hills. To the south, there was another barren area where sparse new growth softened the acres of stumps and raw soil left behind by loggers. But beyond that, a dense forest stood like a dark wall guarding a more natural place that was separated from the rest of the world. We had passed those woods on our way to Gull Walk.

No one was in sight anywhere. Overhead, gulls drifted idly. Beneath them, the water rippled a little, hinting at unseen currents. I had never felt more alone. I was like one of those blue glass balls used to keep fishing nets afloat that sometimes broke loose and floated far away, to wash up on strange beaches. Meg and I had found one once, in happier times when it never occurred to me to look ahead and wonder what might happen to me.

I skidded down the low cliff, sat with my lemonade glass beside me, and leaned back against a driftwood snag. Gulls called to each other, and the tide whispered as it retreated down the rocky, sloping beach, sounding almost as if it were whispering the first letters of my name. *Shh, shh, shh.* I closed my eyes, turning my face toward the sun.

Suddenly I *knew* something was watching me. I turned quickly, expecting to see the cat behind me. But he wasn't there. I held my breath, listening, looking around, but I was alone.

I had fallen into a light doze in the afternoon sunlight when Will slid down the sandy bank and dropped beside me. "I washed," he said loudly as he picked up a stone and threw it toward a tangle of seaweed near the water. The stone fell short and a spindly-legged shorebird took off, peeping angrily at the disturbance.

"Sorry," Will told the bird, but the bird flapped away with one final, outraged squeak.

I pushed my glasses up in place and examined Will. "You washed half of your face and a couple of fingers," I said, sighing and getting to my feet. I shook sand off my wrinkled skirt, picked up the lemonade glass, and said, "Come on, Will. You can scrub the dirt off at the faucet under the porch."

Will loved a faucet wash at Gull Walk, which made no sense to me. The water was always so cold, and it tasted faintly of moss, as if it had been pumped from a forest spring. But it was slightly rusty, too. Like everything else about the guesthouse, it indicated years of neglect. Years of waiting for something to happen that never did.

"I was supposed to tell you that dinner is ready," Will said as we turned to the road that led back to Gull

Walk. "It's some kind of stew on noodles, but it won't be as good as Mom makes." His narrow face saddened, and I thought that it was like seeing the sun slip away.

I slung my arm around his bony shoulders—he was so small for his age! —and hugged him. "We'll be having Mama's good food next year," I said. "Maybe we'll even be able to go to Hawaii and stay with Dad. Think of that. I wonder what the people who live there like to eat."

"I don't want to go there," Will said. He was about to say more when Jonah caught up with us, appearing suddenly out of the old orchard where the grass grew knee-deep and hummed with bees. With his grimy big paw, he held out a dozen red and yellow cherries to Will.

"Here, eat something," Jonah said. "You're so skinny that I can hardly see you when you turn sideways."

He did not offer cherries to me, and even though I did not like Jonah, I still felt a small pang of disappointment. But Will held up one to me by the stem and smiled when I took it.

Jonah had been good to Will from their first day at Gull Walk, when he sat for an hour on the porch with him that evening, murmuring about all the things he would be seeing—the animals in the forest, the birds, and sometimes even orcas in the Sound that visited at high tide, so close to the beach that one could make out their individual white markings. Now he told Will about a pheasant he had seen in the orchard, and Will was listening more attentively than he ever did to anyone else.

I did my best to revise my opinion of the stringy, untidy Jonah, but it was impossible. Even chiding myself by remembering that he had been orphaned like Will, and lived on the charity of the Warders, did nothing to soften my disapproval. Apparently he felt the same way about me. What little he had said to me since we arrived had been rude, sometimes bordering on bullying. He was inclined to making comments like "Get out of my way, Four Eyes," and "What are you staring at, stupid?" and running off before I could retaliate—which I longed to do.

Will scrubbed under the faucet, wiped his hands and face dry on his shirttail, and the two of us went inside, to join the others in the small breakfast room off the main dining room. This room, cheery enough even though the gold and cream striped wallpaper had curled around the edges and the brown carpet was worn through to the warp, was used just by us, with the Warders serving their guests, the Fletchers, in the big dining room near the fireplace. After dinner, the Warders would eat at one end of the cluttered kitchen table.

Helen sat at the head of our table, since she was the oldest, and Meg sat at the foot. Will and I sat on one side, and bashful blond Scotty sat on the other. There was another mismatched chair for Jonah, but he seldom showed up for meals and was bad mannered enough not to apologize. The Warders let him get away with everything, showering him with approval and affection no matter what he did—or did not do. He was absent again, and Scotty looked disappointed.

I shook out my napkin and spread it over my lap. Will imitated me, grinning across at Scotty as if they shared a joke. Scotty's light blue eyes squinted and he laughed, wriggling in his chair.

"Sit still, Scotty," Helen said loudly. She looked around the table at the rest of us and said, "Now we'll say grace."

"Bless this meat. Hurry up and eat," Will said, and even Meg laughed, startled.

But then she asked sharply, "Where on earth did you hear that?"

"From Jonah," Will said, grinning.

"Ye gods," I muttered.

"No cursing," Helen announced. "At home, Mother makes anyone who curses put a penny in the missionary box."

"We're not at your house and I haven't got a penny," I said angrily, and I took my first mouthful of the stew that had been served neatly on one side of my plate, next to a sprig of early parsley and—oh horrors!—two slices of boiled beet. The stew really was good, I was starved, and I glanced at Jonah's full plate speculatively. Even when he was there, he never did much more than pick at his food. I could take his leftovers—

but I could always help myself to more in the kitchen. Miss Warder had said so. Surely having such a huge appetite was a healthy sign.

But it just did not seem comfortable, helping myself to more in a strange kitchen when I had not yet earned my keep.

When I was not yet sure I actually had a home.

Helen, apparently giving up the hope of grace before that particular dinner, ate daintily, seasoning the meal with a sprinkling of criticism of the way I had made her bed. "*My* mother taught me to make hospital corners with the sheets," she said, tossing her dark curls so affectedly that I longed to slap her. "We always have hospital corners on the beds at our house, not just big sloppy bunches of sheets hanging over the ends."

"Then make your own bed," I said crossly. I longed to say more, perhaps even swear loudly. I was sick of Helen's bragging about how perfect everything was at home—and preening over her hair. I shoved a large forkful of stew into my mouth and chewed hard with my mouth open, daring to be rude and hoping that Helen was disgusted. Under the table, Will's foot touched mine warningly.

I looked at him quickly, surprised. Since when did Will care about table manners—or arguments in progress, unless he planned to join in? He bent over his plate, seeming to ignore me, but his silky lashes fluttered nervously.

Jonah strolled in then, his hair and shirt wet, looking as if he, too, had washed at the outdoor faucet. "Oh, stew," he said. "Good." He plopped into his chair, ignored his napkin, and stabbed the meat out of the stew with his fork, head lowered, and he made no further effort to join in a conversation.

Not that there was any more conversation. Meg ate silently, not finishing anything, blinking back tears. So there had been no letter that day from Angus, back in Seattle, I thought. Well, it had only been a week since they had said good-bye, and boys probably were not good letter writers.

Or worse yet, Angus truly had been waiting for her to leave so that he could begin dating Bibi, who had no neck and stuffed her bra with tissue paper, something I knew for an absolute fact, since I had been told so by my best friend, Alma, who had witnessed this in the ladies' restroom at church before a Wednesday prayer meeting.

Suddenly I felt Jonah's gaze on me, raspy as sandpaper. I looked up and saw that he was laughing silently, as if he had read my mind.

Oh, how I despise you! I thought furiously, and I could not imagine how I could endure an entire summer with Jonah. Or Helen.

Or anyone except my own immediate family, for that matter.

Chapter 3

Late in the afternoon, the Griffin insisted that a meeting be called, a proper meeting with everyone present, which meant that everyone would have to go to the high meadow. Even the Old Midwife Tree. Only the Dragon could be excused, because he was born but not yet born, and he knew his duty. He would have to wait until someone told him what had been decided. He grumbled, but he never risked his mission. He would come forth only when the Prince arrived.

The Old Midwife Tree was furious, yelling and throwing twigs, but finally she wrenched up her roots and hobbled to the high meadow. The Unicorn followed her, worried and attempting to soothe her, but nothing she said mattered to the Midwife, and the unicorn colt only made everything worse by pretending to hobble the way the Midwife did.

"What is the point?" the Midwife shouted at everyone. "Why have a meeting? It's been years and nothing changes. We are living in a dream invented by toads!"

Half a dozen small creeping things, light orange in color, objected shrilly. They often took the forms of toads, or sometimes frogs, and several times even salamanders, although that was difficult. The Midwife scattered leaves over them contemptuously and labored on. "Pointless!" she cried at the Griffin, who was far ahead.

At last everyone was there—unicorn cousins, the wyvern family, a phoenix and his young nephew who had no respect for anyone and was known to be as impossible as the unicorn colt, the griffin children who were barely old enough to be included in meetings and were inclined to fall asleep when bored, a crowd of noisy Sky Wings, cranky Walking Wings, and so many unruly Spirit Lights that the Fox Fairy and his elderly uncle demanded that they be sent away until they learned good manners. The youngest creatures exasperated their elders by shape-shifting and bickering, and half of them had to be rounded up by their parents and warned sternly to behave or the Dragon would hatch. Since none of the young ones had ever seen a real dragon—the two-legged wyverns did not count— but had only heard the tales of them, they fell quiet at last and sat down to listen.

The Griffin invited the Fox Fairy to tell all of his news. The Fox Fairy concluded speaking by saying, "We must be more willing than ever to take on the Mudwalkers now. I am still quick and strong . . ."

"Enough," the Griffin said wearily. "The hunters have

too much power. There must be no more battles, no matter how we are provoked. There are too few of us and everyone is needed. If the Prince is really nearby—"

"If! If!" the Fox Fairy snapped. "I say that he is here!"

"What if he is? How do you expect to bring him to Darkwood?" someone called out. "The Mudwalkers wouldn't give him up without a fight, not if they know who he is."

"We will kidnap him," the Fox Fairy said confidently. "It won't be hard. And once the Midwife shows him the History, he will stay willingly and help us. Who would not?"

"Mudwalkers would not," several voices said despondently.

"Not all are evil—" the Fox Fairy began.

"Liar!" the Midwife shouted.

"Not all are evil," the Griffin said firmly. "The Guardians are Mudwalkers, and they are good. Or as good as Mudwalkers can be. They have never harmed one of us."

The Midwife snorted. "They're saving you to kill some other day," she said. "They'll shoot you or run over you on the road, and then they'll stuff you and put you on display somewhere in a Mudwalker town."

The Fox Fairy sighed. "Enough of this. We need to agree on a plan. We need to be of one mind."

"Like the Mudwalkers?" the Midwife asked bitterly.

"If that is all that will work," the Griffin said. "They have *defeated us everywhere because they are of one mind. They want to destroy what they do not understand."*

"There is another Mudwalker who might help us," the Fox Fairy mused. "Or, then again, she might hurt us. I haven't decided yet. She could be a Between, and if she knows about the Prince . . ."

"A Between?" the Midwife cried incredulously. "As if I would trust your opinion! Is this meeting over? I'm tired of listening to nonsense and tall tales. If you think you have found the Prince, then produce him."

From Charlotte Thacker's notebook

After dinner, the Fletchers went out for another of their evening walks, although where they went no one knew—or cared. I caught a glimpse of them marching up the road side by side, not speaking, short arms swinging a little, fat feet in their sturdy shoes clopping along. They looked as out of place as soldiers would in the quiet landscape. The Warders did not seem particularly interested in their paying guests, beyond giving them good service. In turn, the Fletchers treated them with barely concealed contempt—and stared rudely at us. I felt that the couple stared longest and hardest at Will, for some reason. Perhaps they had overheard the conversation about Will being adopted. Seeing them leave Gull Walk, if only for a little while, brought me relief.

Jonah was already gone, having rushed out of the room as soon as he finished his dessert. Will shuffled out to the porch swing to read one of the books he had brought from home.

Helen and Meg went upstairs with a movie magazine to try out the latest hairstyles of the Hollywood stars, using the dim mirror in the staff bathroom on the second floor. There was no bathroom in the attic. I had not been invited to join them, but I consoled myself by volunteering to help Miss Warder in the kitchen before the woman had a chance to ask.

Later, tired but satisfied with my voluntary martyr's role—although my hands were puckered and pale from dishwater—I wandered into the shabby sitting room, a place we were not encouraged to use. But the guests were out, so what difference did it make? One evening I might even turn on the radio and see if it worked.

I found Scotty there, sitting on the carpet in front of a small bookcase that held not much more than old copies of *National Geographic* magazine, some with bookmarks, and a world atlas that also held bookmarks, as if someone had been planning a trip once upon a time. The bookmarks were yellowed with age. There was a handful of old novels with broken spines on the shelves, too, and a stack of old magazines crammed in on top of them.

Scotty, paging slowly through a magazine featuring

a rather startled African on the cover, looked up briefly with a small smile.

He did not notice the ladybug creeping down the bookcase, over the magazine spines. I loved ladybugs and was about to bend down to take a closer look when the insect took off, wings busy propelling its bulky red body, and suddenly it *changed*. There was only the slightest blurring of its shape, and then it was—something else. Something much thinner and nearly transparent, a glimmering small form that darted toward the hall and then up the wide stairs toward the second floor.

Amazed, I hesitated, and then I ran after it. Scotty said something behind me, but I did not really hear. Where was the flying creature? *What* was it?

Halfway up the stairs to the landing, I suddenly felt dizzy. My eyes stung, as if sand had blown into them. Or as if I had seen something I had not been meant to see. I took off my glasses and clasped one hand over my eyes. From above, Jonah's voice asked, "What's wrong with *you*, Four Eyes?"

I took away my hand and peered painfully at him. "Nothing," I said, nearly choking on my quick anger. Four Eyes! Who did he think he was, with his big dirty bare feet and ragged overalls? "What are you doing up here?"

"Taking out the trash basket in the Fletchers' room," he said, too easily. He held the basket behind his back, as if he did not want me to see what it contained. But I did not care anything about the Fletchers or what they might have discarded. Perhaps Jonah had stolen something from their room. I did not care about that either.

Jonah ran past me down the stairs and I climbed the rest of them to my room. Did I look sick? I did not want anyone wondering about me. There was nothing to worry about. And who would not have felt worn out after cleaning the kitchen, almost without help from Miss Warder? No, in all fairness, that was not true. Miss Warder had done the pots, always the worst job, the one I hated most.

And she had told me that I was already worth more than any of the kitchen help they had ever had, in the good old days when the guesthouse was full all summer.

I *am* needed, I told myself as I stretched out on the bed, close to the window where the quiet, cold wind blew off the Sound in the gathering dark. I heard the faint bickering of distant birds, and I could smell salt water and firs and perhaps the even fainter scent of sweet peas. My eyes did not hurt anymore, and whatever I had seen—or had thought I had seen—on the stairs was the product of my imagination and exhaustion.

After a while, Meg and Will came upstairs to bed. Will always fell asleep easily, curled on one side, his hands folded under his chin. But often he would wake a few hours later, shouting and weeping, struggling with anyone who tried to help him. No one could understand what he said, and in the morning he would always insist that he could not remember.

Meg and I had not slept well since we arrived at Gull Walk. There was too much to worry about, Meg had said one night, and I certainly agreed with that.

Also, I had thought that there was too much to listen to outside. At home in Seattle, in our house on a peaceful side street, there were few night noises. Oh, an occasional barking dog and a rare passing car might disturb the gentle quiet. But nothing more. But here, at Gull Walk, the night was filled with sounds— the whisper of water on sand, the sharp yaps and yodels of coyotes, owls giving warning, and occasional high-pitched cries, as if some poor hapless creature had been caught.

Miserable and tossing restlessly, I wondered that night about the people who had rented our Seattle house. They had been quarrelsome, unreasonable people, demanding that the house be fumigated twice before they would agree to a reduced rent. "Germs," they had complained, looking outraged, as if our mother had become ill to spite them and for no other reason. "Somebody was sick here. We could all die." Humiliating conversation followed humiliating conversation, until I had longed to walk straight into the house from the porch where Meg and I had been eavesdropping and insist that these finicky people, whose lout of a son picked his nose right in front of God and everybody, should take themselves out of there and go back where they had come from.

Meg, as if reading my mind there in the dark bedroom, whispered, "We'll be moving back home soon, Charlotte. Our house is only rented out for a year. Mom will get well and Dad will be transferred back to Seattle. There won't be a war, and he'll get out of the Navy again. Everything will be fine."

I sighed.

"But then, of course, *we'll* have to fumigate because of the nose-picker," Meg said softly, and I, surprised, burst out laughing. Will stirred on his cot, moaned, and slept again.

The night wind blew the curtains idly. Outside, I heard the distant beach sounds, one sudden loud bird cry—and something else. Quick feet on the road. An urgent whisper. The thud of—wood against wood? Clubs?

I shivered and pulled the blankets close under my chin. Whatever was there could take care of its own business. I did not want to know what it was. Or who it was.

God bless and heal Mama, I prayed. God keep Daddy safe.

God keep *us* safe, because now I'm afraid that this is a bad place.

Finally I slept, and I dreamed of Gull Walk's true name, but when I awoke in the foggy morning, I had forgotten it.

The first living thing I saw in the morning was the stray cat, sitting on the windowsill. Before I could say anything, he slipped out, murmuring, "You hear too much, but I'll have to trust you. Say nothing to anyone." I heard him leap to the porch roof below the window and patter away busily, as if he were late for a meeting.

Meg woke, mumbled something about dreaming that the country had gone to war with Hitler, and Will jumped up with a glad shout and a big stretch.

"Race you down to the bathroom," he told us.

"Too late," Meg said gloomily. "I just heard Helen going down the stairs."

Sunday at Gull Walk had begun.

We ate cold cereal and fruit in the small breakfast room, while Miss Warder prepared pancakes and eggs for the complaining Fletchers, who had rejected the waffles she had served first.

"Fog again!" I heard Mr. Fletcher say loudly, as if somehow the owners of Gull Walk were responsible. "There is fog nearly every morning this summer. I don't remember it being like that before."

"It's always like this early in summer," his wife said,

but her voice was not soothing. It carried an edge that pummeled listeners so that they would remember forever that she knew everything and intended to have the final word on every subject. "And it's always like this when we come in the fall, too. I don't know why we bother coming when we do in the fall, because it's too early for hunting. Nothing ever happens. Why aren't the Warders open during the hunting season? It's so selfish of them! We always end up staying in that place that only has a coffee shop instead of a proper dining room."

"Quiet!" Mr. Fletcher said sharply. I heard a cup scrape on a saucer, nothing more.

I looked at Meg and saw that Meg was looking straight back at me. One corner of her mouth quirked. Will's foot found my ankle again. Nudge nudge.

"Hey, Will, you want to try out my bike this morning?" Jonah said suddenly. He had surprised us by showing up that morning, and this was the first thing he'd said. "I'll show you a place that most people don't know about. We can ride double."

"No," Meg said firmly. "Riding double is dangerous. Will can't do that."

Jonah groaned. "Aw, for Pete's sake. I won't let the kid get hurt. He can ride on the rack in back, not the handlebars."

"I said no," Meg repeated firmly.

"Then he can ride and I'll run alongside," Jonah said.

I looked up and studied Jonah's face to see if he was lying. I could not tell. "Will, you know better than to do something we told you not to do," I said.

Will nodded eagerly. "I know! I won't ride double. Jonah and I can take turns running alongside."

"Or maybe Mr. Warder will let us use his old bike," Jonah said.

I tried to imagine Mr. Warder on a bike and failed. I laughed. "He has a bike?"

"Oh, sure, for when the car breaks down. It breaks down a lot." Jonah scraped back his chair and caught Mr. Warder passing in the hall.

Mr. Warder agreed easily to loaning his bike, then popped his head in the door. "But how about all of you riding into town with me when I pick up the Sunday papers? Wouldn't that be more fun?"

I saw Will and Jonah exchange a look. Suddenly Will smiled innocently at Mr. Warder and said, "That would be nice. We'd like that."

So it was agreed. All would go except Jonah, and I saw him run off without another word, scowling murderously over his failed plan. Even drooping Meg, doomed to another day without mail, agreed to go, and we set off as soon as the Fletchers finished their breakfast and left for places unknown.

The fog had thickened, and I barely could see the hood ornament on the car when we drove carefully under the dripping trees, down the long driveway to the road. But Mr. Warder assured us that he would honk his horn frequently and drive slowly once we got underway, and we would all have a wonderful time climbing the hill toward town, when we would find that we would be above the fog and out in the sunshine. Gull Walk sat in a little hollow, he said. The fog hung on there longer than in other places.

It was as if Gull Walk needed to be hidden from everybody, I thought sourly. What a place! I hated riding in fog—although walking in it could be exciting. Things loomed out of fog, almost unidentifiable until one was practically on top of them. Anything was possible. Any adventure might begin, while one walked in fog.

Meg and Helen were silent, looking out windows at absolutely nothing, because of the glimmering mist that surrounded us and pressed against the car. Bored, Scotty fell asleep. Will whistled an odd tune under his breath.

Mr. Warder was right. We drove up and out of the fog and by the time we reached town, we traveled in bright sunlight. Mr. Warder parked near the bus station and everyone leaped out, stretching like young animals released from cages. Inside the station, Mr. Warder greeted his friend at the counter and chose two Seattle papers and one from Olympia. Meg had caught the attention of a pair of sailors waiting on a bench, and she blushed and fussed with her hair, to Helen's obvious disgust. Mr. Warder noticed and laughed. But he did not linger inside and asked Meg to carry the papers for him.

Back in the car, he gave the funnies to the boys and the homemaking sections to Meg and Helen. I got the front pages of the *Seattle Times*, handed over to me with a wink. "You look like somebody who enjoys reading the news," he told me.

I did and I did not. I was interested in what went on in the world, but I hated reading about the wars in Europe and Asia. It seemed as if the entire human race had lost its collective mind and was determined to destroy not only itself but every living thing on the planet as well.

I put the paper aside and looked out the car window as we descended the hill, back down into the fog, and finally reaching the driveway of Gull Walk. Something ran in front of the car and Mr. Warder braked suddenly.

"What was that?" I cried. It had been a large creature, larger than a deer, but as long-legged.

"A deer," Mr. Warder said calmly. But when he got out of the car, he banged his door a couple of times, pretending that it had not closed properly the first time, as if he wanted to frighten off the strange beast.

Or warn it.

I tried to peer through the fog as if I might see clearly if only I squinted hard enough through my glasses. "I don't think it was a deer."

Meg and Helen had been looking at the papers, they

said, and they had not seen anything. Scotty only seemed bewildered by the sudden stop. But Will had shrunk inside his jacket, as if trying to make himself smaller.

"Did you see it, Will?" I asked. Will shook his head.

"It was an elk, maybe," Mr. Warder said. "Sometimes we still see a few. They haven't all been killed yet."

Hunters. I shuddered and followed him into the house. I had intended to ask about hunting in the area, but then decided not to do it. Of course there were hunters. There were always hunters. And animals must be killed in wars, too, when their forests were destroyed. But I could not bear to think about it.

Meg and Helen settled themselves in the big attic bedroom with the sections of the papers that carried the Hollywood gossip columns and fashion news. Scotty returned to the sitting room, where he gathered up an armload of magazines and carried them upstairs to his small room, and Will joined him, murmuring something about South America and jungles.

"How do you know about the jungles there?" I heard Scotty asking Will as I passed their doorway. "Have you ever seen one?"

"Somebody told me about them," Will said.

I joined the other girls and stretched out on Will's cot, yanking his pillow behind my head.

"Are you sure you didn't see that animal that ran past the car when we got here?" I asked them.

Meg and Helen looked up from the newspaper. "No," Meg said. "Who cares? We didn't hit it."

"Mr. Warder said it was a deer or an elk," Helen said.

I lay very still, waiting for something—I didn't know what—with my heart beating a little too hard. "It didn't have antlers."

"Maybe it was a female," Meg said absentmindedly as she turned a page. "I don't think they have antlers."

"Right." Helen rolled over on her stomach and examined the page that Meg was reading. "Look at that hat, Meg. Do you like it?"

I closed my eyes and tried to remember exactly what I had seen when we reached the house. The boys, who had been sitting in front with Mr. Warder, should have seen the creature! They were practically on top of it!

Well, Scotty could have fallen asleep over his comics. But Will . . .

My brother who had no shadow.

Suddenly I was certain that Will knew exactly what had run across the driveway in the fog.

The day dragged on as if it had been chained to my ankle, not letting me move into the future where I longed to be, with a reunited family and Will his own self again.

Finally we went down to help Miss Warder in the kitchen. The Fletchers were back, drinking coffee in the dining room and reading the newspapers. Both looked up when I walked through to the kitchen. I nodded, but they did not. Their eyes were hard and watchful, as if they had a reason not to trust me.

Immediately I remembered Jonah coming out of their room with their wastebasket. Had he taken something?

I would hear about it if he had. Perhaps even be blamed for it.

Miss Warder was testing a roast beef to see if it was done. Potatoes were lined up in another oven, baking. The sink was full of salad vegetables, and she had baked a chocolate cake.

"If you girls would set the tables, I'd be grateful," she said as she shoved the roasting pan back in the oven.

"Do you want flowers again?" I asked.

"Yes, dear, if you would."

I took the scissors out of the drawer and let myself out the back door quietly. The fog had thinned a little, and I could hear the lapping water on the shore. The air smelled heavy with the scents of seaweed—and some wild animal scent I could not identify.

I made my way carefully down the back steps, slick with moisture from the fog, and reached for an especially nice red sweet pea.

"Things could move swiftly now," the cat said from under the porch.

I froze. The cat moved closer to the lattice. "Keep your mouth shut," he said. "No one will believe you anyway." And then he moved back, out of sight.

I stood very still for a long time. My mind was blank. And then I gathered sweet peas as if nothing had happened because I did not know what else to do.

People do not go crazy this way, I told myself. But how would I know? The only crazy person I had ever met was my fourth-grade teacher who had gone mad one afternoon and thrown a chair through a window. Not one student moved or made a sound. The teacher had rushed out then, and after a while the principal came in and finished the class with us, saying nothing about what had happened. The teacher never came back, and no explanation was ever given. My parents, upset at first, finally explained that sometimes people had too many burdens and reacted strangely. I was not to worry—so I didn't.

But people did not hear talking cats, except for Alice in Wonderland, and that happened in a book. Everybody knew that the things in books were not always true. Not always.

I made an especially nice bouquet of flowers and ferns for the Fletchers' table—certainly a much nicer bouquet than an insane person would make—and then I helped Meg and Helen with the salads.

But late that night, after everyone else had fallen asleep, I watched while Will sat up in bed and juggled a ball of glimmering lights between his hands. After a while the ball separated into a hundred individual lights, and the small creatures like the one I had seen before fluttered out the open window and disappeared, chattering shrilly, into the darkness.

And Will lay down to sleep. That night he did not have a nightmare.

But I did. I dreamed that I stood in a deep forest and watched strange animals watching me. When I ran away, they did not follow because they already knew my name.

Chapter 4

The Fox Fairy lay down with a sigh next to the Old Midwife Tree, and she said, "What's wrong now? Have you been stirring up trouble? Fighting again?"

"Certainly not," he said. Then he added, "Well, I didn't start it."

"You start everything," the Midwife said. "You agreed that there was to be no more trouble."

"I was merely strolling down the road," he argued. "How was I to know Mudwalkers would see me?"

"You were playing tricks again!" she cried furiously, and she showered him with twigs and leaves. "They see you when you want them to see you. What were you this time? A two-headed snake? A naked Mudwalker carrying a club?"

He stood and shook the rubbish off his fur. "All that really matters is that I am sure now that the Prince is here, with the Guardians. And he is beginning to remember."

"What proof do you have, other than your imagining that you can call his shadow?"

"I do *call* his shadow!" the Fox Fairy cried angrily. "I call and it comes. And the Prince is beginning to remember."

The Midwife was silent, thinking. She rustled a branch, then said, "How can you be sure?"

"He plays with Spirit Lights. They understand each other. It is the same with the Sky Wing Spirits—they speak together. One of the Mudwalker children found maps in books, and the Prince has been studying them and asking the Sky Wing Spirits questions."

The Midwife gasped. "Have they given him news of the other Darkwoods?"

"No," the Fox Fairy said. "He is not ready for that yet."

The Midwife was silent for a long time then. Finally she said, "It has been a long time since most of the Sky Wing Spirits made the long journeys. They are too weak. Are you sure they are not inventing stories to make themselves seem important? They are vain and stupid creatures . . ."

A shrill protest arose from the nest, and a Sky Wing Spirit sat on the edge of it, scolding the Midwife.

"All right, all right," she said. "Do be quiet."

"There is more," the Fox Fairy said. "Some of the Mudwalkers who are staying with the Guardians suspect that the Prince is here."

The Midwife thrashed her branches. "Nonsense! You said they were only children!"

"Not all of them. Can't you remember anything? There are two old ones who have been here before. They received a message from another Mudwalker, saying that he would come to help them soon. And I am sure now that one of the children is a Between, like the Guardians."

"A Between! I don't believe you," the Old Midwife Tree said.

"I talk to her and she answers."

The Old Midwife laughed. "Ridiculous! When you take on the Mudwalker form, of course she can hear you!"

"She hears me as the cat—and you know that only the Betweens can hear animals speak," the Fox Fairy said. "She hears!"

The Old Midwife mulled this over. "You'd better tell the others then."

The Fox Fairy nodded and slipped away.

From Charlotte Thacker's notebook

I lay awake most of the night, wishing that I trusted my sister enough to confide in her. Wishing I trusted anyone! But there was no way I could explain the things that had been happening so that they would seem convincing. I considered questioning Will—but what if I had been imagining everything? Even Will would think I had lost my mind. Certainly I would think the same thing if anyone told me about a talking cat and sparks that seemed to be alive and a ladybug that changed shape.

The long night finally passed. Gray dawn—fog again! —pressed against the window, and I finally slept.

I awoke when Meg jumped out of bed and rushed downstairs to the bathroom to take a quick bath, before Helen could monopolize the tub. Will struggled to sit up on his cot, yawning and blinking, and I took advantage of this. "What were those sparks you were playing with last night?" I asked quickly, before he was fully awake.

"Spirit Lights," he said, and he yawned again. "From Darkwood."

Then he blinked and stared at me. "I don't know what you're talking about," he said hastily.

"Too late," I said. "I saw you."

Will made a great pretense of being sleepy, yawned again, groaned, and lay back down. "I'm still tired. I can't talk now."

I got out of bed, grabbed my robe and the small bag that contained my toothbrush and comb, and hurried out of the room. "I saw *everything*," I said from the doorway. "And I won't forget it, either."

Will muttered something I could not hear, but I did not stop and go back. So I had not been imagining anything. Something was wrong with Will. Wrong or different or special. *Something.* But what would I do about it?

This was frightening information to hold all alone.

Helen stood outside the staff bathroom door, carrying her own toiletry bag, and Scotty sat on the floor beside her, half asleep, clutching a worn teddy bear. "You have to wait in line," Helen said, as if I did not wait in line every single morning.

I felt as if the top of my head was about to come off. I was furious and frightened, and suddenly this unwanted stay at Gull Walk seemed like the worst sort of punishment for a crime I did not know I had committed, especially since I was not certain yet that my parents had any idea where we were. So I said loudly, "No, I *won't* wait in line. There are two other bathrooms on this floor and I'm going to use one of them!"

"They're for guests!" Helen cried. "You aren't supposed to go in them. Miss Warder said so."

"I don't care!" I shouted.

One bathroom was used by the Fletchers, so I chose the other one, halfway down the hall. I went in and banged the door behind me. It was a much nicer bathroom than the one we had been given. The floor was shiny yellow tile, not linoleum, and the tub was larger. The towels, only a trifle musty, were thicker and whiter. I put the rubber plug in the tub drain, turned on the hot water, and watched with satisfaction while the tub filled with steaming water. Someone knocked on the door, but I shouted, "Go away!"

"You're going to get into trouble," Helen singsonged.

I did not need to see her to know she was smirking.

"Who cares!" I cried furiously. Someday, I thought, I'll get something on Helen and then won't she pay for how she's treated me! But I was wearing myself out for nothing, and I knew it. I heard her stomping away and I stuck out my tongue, wishing she could see *that!*

Ah. Deliciously hot water. I stripped off my nightgown and slipped into the tub, sinking down until even my head was covered. When I came up, I knew I was smiling. I soaped my hair with the new scented bar from the soap dish and sank under the water again. The scent was too strong, smelling almost violently of roses, but I did not care. I worked up a massive heap of suds before finally climbing out of the tub, and, wrapped in a towel, watched while the water drained out of the tub but the suds did not. Someone would have to clean it up, but it was not going to be me!

Clad only in my robe, I marched back upstairs to the attic to dress. Meg, buttoning her favorite cotton shirt, said, "Helen told me what you did, but I can't believe it. Do you want to get us into trouble?"

I began dressing inside my robe in case Will walked in. "I can't believe I did it, either. But Helen was ahead of me and she takes forever in the bathroom, and I get so tired of waiting. I'm tired of everything! What are we doing here, anyway?" I struggled to keep from crying, and then shouted, "Mama and Dad don't even know where we are!"

Meg stared at me. "What on earth is wrong with you? You act as if you're going crazy."

"I'm not crazy!" I cried, scrubbing tears from my face and wiping my nose with the sleeve on my robe.

If Meg only knew what had been going on! But she must not find out. Meg, the letter writer, could not be trusted with a secret—ever.

Meg, Helen, and I went down to help Miss Warder in the kitchen, and if the woman knew anything about my bath rebellion, she did not say so. Our breakfast was cold cereal, juice, and toast. Jonah, as usual, was absent, but I had seen him through the window, sitting on the back porch swing whittling on a stick, as if that were more important than anything else in the world.

Scotty and Will talked about comics at the table. Helen stared at me but said nothing. Meg looked as if she wished she were somewhere else. Well, who didn't?

The fog cleared away before noon, to be replaced with a steady drizzle blowing ahead of a cold wind that tossed seagulls high above the beach. The Fletchers, complaining, left after their late breakfast of eggs and bacon, and told Mr. Warder, who had been serving them, that they would not return until bedtime. They offered no explanation, and Mr. Warder looked as if he was pleased that he would not be burdened with one. He went to town shortly afterward, for the mail, and he took Jonah with him. Miss Warder busied herself on the second floor, making up the Fletchers' room—and perhaps discovering the sacrilege in the previously unused bathroom. I tried to tell myself that I did not care, but a knot of worry lodged in my stomach and did not leave. My temper outbursts always left me sorry—but regret never cured me of them, either.

Will avoided me. When I walked into the sitting room, where he had been looking at magazines with Scotty, Will got up and left without saying a word. Well, let him try to avoid me! Sooner or later he would have to answer questions, and I had plenty of them.

I picked up the magazine he had been reading. It did not seem particularly interesting. A bookmark was stuck between two pages of black-and-white photographs of a jungle somewhere in South America, a place never photographed before, according to the legend under one of the pictures. I peered closely at the trees, saw little to care about, and put the magazine back on the shelf.

"What are you reading?" I asked Scotty.

He held up his magazine, open at a bookmark. Another jungle. "I can only read some of the words. Tell me what this says."

I read the caption aloud. Apparently this was the first photo ever taken of that jungle, too, and no one knew how many different kinds of animals lived there. Curious, I opened the magazine at another bookmark. Sure enough, there was a photo of other thick trees growing somewhere in another part of the world.

"Do you want to travel all over the world when you grow up?" I asked Scotty. I was not particularly interested but only wanted something to say.

He shook his head. "I just want to go home."

"So do I," I said.

The mail brought letters for everyone, and we gathered in our small breakfast room to share news from family and friends. Helen, barely able to sit still, told us that her mother and new baby brother had come home from the hospital—and both of them were fine. "But Dad says we have to stay here for a few weeks while Mom rests."

I also had received a short letter from Uncle Ned, in which he explained that he had called the hospital where Mama was staying and had been told that she was not any worse. "I'm waiting to hear from your father," he concluded.

So am I, I thought sadly. Why didn't Dad write? Surely a letter would have reached me by now. But what if it had been mailed to the Tates' house? What happened to letters sent to the wrong place?

I also received a thick letter from Alma, which I saved to read later, by myself. Will smiled over a postcard that one of his classmates sent to him, and he seemed content enough. He actually seemed normal, and I suffered a moment of self-doubt that made me sick to my stomach. Scotty received a card from his mother, telling him about his new brother, whose name was Timothy.

But Meg was not happy. There was no letter from Angus, which did not surprise me. However, she had received a long letter from her best friend, and she read it quickly, then went back to the beginning and read it all over again. She blinked rapidly and bit her lower lip.

"So what's new with Connie?" I asked as I stuffed Alma's letter into my pocket.

"Nothing much," Meg said. She got to her feet abruptly and left the room. Moments later we heard her footsteps pounding up the stairs, all the way to the attic. A door slammed.

"I guess she got bad news about her boyfriend," Helen said. I could detect a glint of satisfied malice in her eyes.

Half a dozen angry answers nearly spilled out of my mouth, but I said nothing. I did not want to spend the day bickering with Helen, no matter how tempting it might be. Instead, I went to the kitchen to see if I could be of help there. Sometimes the best thing to do was work. Then you did not think so much.

Miss Warder was chopping vegetables for soup, and my mouth watered. "I love homemade soup," I said. "Is there anything I can do?"

"If you'd finish the rest of the dirty dishes, I'd be

grateful," Miss Warder said. "How do you feel about staying here? You don't say much."

"It's nice here. I like the woods and being so close to the Sound."

"You should have seen it years ago, when my brother and I were children," Miss Warder said. She looked out the window wistfully. "The forest came up close to Gull Walk then. It was filled with wonderful wildlife. Deer sometimes came and looked in our windows, as if we were fish in a bowl." She laughed, remembering. "But that was before the town grew so large. Before—"

"Before what?" I asked. I rinsed a plate in hot water and put it in the rack.

The silence lasted a moment too long, and then Miss Warder said, "Before most of the trees were cut down. And we learned a painful lesson."

I waited for Miss Warder to elaborate, but she changed the subject instead. "It's hard staying inside on a rainy day, but with a good umbrella, you might enjoy strolling around for a while. When you're finished, I mean. See how different the Sound looks—how different everything looks. Rain is so healing."

I, who walked six blocks to school back in Seattle, did not think of rain as anything but bad news. "I didn't bring an umbrella," I said.

"We have several," she said. "You and your sister might find a stroll to your liking."

I doubted if Meg would find anything to her liking on

that day. "Maybe Will and Scotty could go."

"Not Will!" Miss Warder exclaimed. She had whirled around to face me, and her face had gone white.

I stared. "Why not?" I asked finally, amazed at her reaction.

I could see Miss Warder struggling to find words—or invent an excuse for her exclamation. Does she know something? I wondered, horrified. Had she seen Will's shadow or the ball of sparks? This was not good.

Miss Warder turned back to her cutting board. Her hands were trembling a little. "He's not as big as he should be at his age. Ned told us he was a sickly child. We don't want to take the chance of his catching a chill."

Without thinking, I blurted, "He doesn't have TB! We were all tested and X-rayed."

"I didn't mean that," Miss Warder said quickly. "Of course he doesn't have TB. All of you are going to be fine. I only meant that he is rather small and frail for his age, and since I'm responsible for him, I don't want him outside in bad weather. You can understand that."

My anger seeped away. I had to stop being so sensitive about the subject of tuberculosis. Nothing was wrong with my brother.

Nothing was wrong with him? I could have laughed if the subject had not been so serious.

I scrubbed ferociously at a spot on a plate. Something *is* wrong with Will, I thought. He doesn't always have a shadow! He plays with little sparks of lights and calls them "spirits." What is going to happen to him? To all of us?

When I finished my work, I looked in on Will and Scotty, who were playing checkers in Scotty's room while Helen read a book. The scene was peaceful enough. There were no sparks in the air, and the overhead light revealed Will's shadow exactly where it should be.

I crossed the hall to my bedroom, dreading facing Meg. But we were sisters, and if Meg was unhappy, then I must try to help.

I found her facedown on the bed, and pages of Connie's letter were scattered on the floor. Some of them had been wadded up into little balls. Meg looked up when I entered.

"Oh, it's just you," she said, and she buried her face in her pillow again. Her eyelids were swollen and red, and she had a crumpled handkerchief in one hand.

I sat on my own side of the bed. "I'm sorry if Connie told you something that makes you sad. Was it about Angus?"

"He goes to Bibi's house every single day and then walks to the beach with her. He's even taking her to the midsummer dance."

"Who says so?" I demanded.

Meg shrugged. "Connie. She says everybody knows."

"Gee, what a friend," I said disgustedly. "You'd be better off with warts."

63

"Well, somebody had to tell me!" Meg cried. "I knew Angus and Bibi were . . . Oh, why does everything bad happen to us?"

I had no answer. Everything bad *was* happening to us. But I thought that Meg did not know the worst of it yet. *Will.*

"Would you like to go for a walk?" I asked. "Miss Warder has umbrellas we can use."

"In the rain?" Meg cried. "I can't think of anything I'd hate more than that."

I told Meg again that I was sorry about the bad news in Connie's letter and went back downstairs. Rain or not, I needed to get away where I could think.

Miss Warder took a big black umbrella out of the closet near the front door, and she told me to visit the beach or walk to the big dairy farm farther down the road.

"I thought I'd go in the other direction," I said. "Toward what's left of the forest."

"Oh, no, you don't want to go there," Miss Warder said quickly, shaking her head. "Nobody does. There's nothing to see, believe me."

Outside, I opened the umbrella and listened to the rain pelt it. It made a good sound, comforting and maybe even a little romantic. So where should I go? Down to the beach or to the dairy farm?

Neither. A rebellious impulse shoved me toward the last of the old forest. The umbrella was so large that it shut out a view of almost everything, but once I caught a glimpse of someone ahead of me, a boy on a bike, pedaling hard to make it up the hill.

Jonah?

It *was* Jonah. Where was he going?

But I had no hope of keeping up with him, even though the road here was too steep for Jonah to pedal very fast. As I grew nearer the woods, I saw that there was a barbed wire fence around them, at least along the road and down the edge of a long field dotted with stumps and young alders. "No Hunting!" and "Keep Out!" signs had been put up on the posts.

And then I saw Jonah's bike, lying on its side in the grass beside the road. Jonah was nowhere around. He must have taken the risk of climbing the fence so he could go into the woods. But why, on a wet day like this?

I turned back. Rain was falling harder now and my shoes were soaked.

"She's leaving," someone whispered. "Leaving, leaving . . ."

I stopped, looked around, saw no one, and began running, terrified. That had not been a human voice, at least not like any human I had ever known.

Chapter 5

The Griffin joined the Fox Fairy under the Midwife Tree and sighed. "The weather is bad and the children living with the Guardians have been staying indoors most of the time. I have not had an opportunity to decide whether or not the Prince is there."

The Fox Fairy snorted. "I knew him better than you did. I would recognize him anywhere, all the way to the end of the world, even if he has changed into a Mudwalker shape. He is clumsy and noisy like them now, but there is no way a true Fair Prince could lose his noble ways."

"It has happened before," The Old Midwife said mournfully. "Long ago, a Sky Wing told me that she had seen a Fair One who had grown to old age without knowing her true identity. She spent her time searching woods without knowing what she hoped to find."

"She didn't recognize any of us?" the Griffin asked, horrified. "She looked but she did not see? She never learned that she was a Fair One?"

"She never found a Darkwood. She only walked in the damaged forests where we had been driven out."

"But there have been Mudwalkers before who have tried to disguise themselves as Fair Ones," the Old Midwife said. "As Princes and Princesses, even. They will never stop trying to destroy us. We cannot take chances. Oh, fire and storm blast the evil day that the Chimera made the first Mudwalkers and their animals. For a joke, he said! Just for a game! He said they were only toys! But he knew exactly what he was doing, and the Old Dragon was right to destroy him for it."

"Stop, stop! I swear to you by everything sacred—even by the Dragon!—that the young Mudwalker I've seen is really our Prince," the Fox Fairy cried, exasperated.

"Then bring him here and let us judge for ourselves," the Old Midwife Tree said.

The Griffin nodded. "I am afraid she is right. All here must see for themselves, and all must agree that he is the Prince. Otherwise, it is too dangerous. If we are seen as ourselves by one of the Mudwalkers, you know that they will come to destroy our Darkwood—and us. The Chimera planned it, and even though he is dead, his plan still unfolds."

The young Dragon in his egg at the bottom of the pond yawned and said, "Bring the boy here to look down into the water. If he is only a Mudwalker, he will see a Mudwalker. But if he is a Prince, then he will see a Prince. Now go away."

From Charlotte Thacker's notebook

Rain fell all week, a cold and drenching rain that poured day and night, and we were trapped indoors, where even the carpets and wallpaper seemed to be absorbing the damp. Lights burned all day in the downstairs rooms and did very little to dispel my feelings of being caught in a perpetual twilight.

Early in the week, the disgusted Fletchers announced that they were going to Portland to visit friends and would return on the following Monday. Overhearing this, I was not sure whether to be relieved or sorry. They were unpleasant people, but at least they were people, other inhabitants in the building. No one else came to stay. Except for Mr. Warder's daily trip to town for the newspapers, mail, and odds and ends of groceries, the days dragged. Sometimes one of us went with him, but most of the time the trip sounded too dismal to even attempt.

Miss Warder allowed us to use the radio in the sitting room, although she warned us that we were never to listen to news programs because they were too depressing for children. We would have avoided them anyway, because broadcasters only wanted to talk about the wars—and the inevitability of the United States being involved in them. Even I, who once was interested in happenings around the world, turned the radio dial quickly if someone began discussing reality. I stopped reading the front pages of newspapers, too. Life was hard enough without dwelling on catastrophies.

But Meg and Helen promptly located soap operas on the radio and sat close by, listening intently and occasionally arguing quietly about the plots. Did "Ma Perkins" interfere too much in the lives of others? Wasn't "Stella Dallas" just too foolish? Were "Vic and Sade" real people? I sat across the room pretending to read. The other two girls, not all that much older than I, had formed an exclusive friendship—for a while at least—and I wanted them to believe that I did not care. With the way things were going at Gull Walk, it was only a matter of time before they were arguing with each other again.

Will and Scotty, too far apart in years to be truly close friends, tried to play board games on the table in the breakfast room, but Will always won, unless he deliberately let Scotty win, and then Scotty would end up tearful and cross. By Wednesday, no one wanted to get up in the morning, and no one was willingly speaking to anyone else. Doors slammed a lot, and certain people became expert at sighing dramatically in the silences.

Jonah appeared for lunch and dinner, ate rapidly, and vanished. If he had a room of his own in Gull Walk, I did not know where it was and did not care to ask. Perhaps he slept in the basement, near the furnace. He always looked grimy and disheveled. He never seemed to change clothes.

Will now seemed like a completely normal boy. He had a shadow and he did not play with the things that looked like living sparks. The talking cat had not been back. If the bad weather was responsible for these improvements, I supposed that I should be grateful, but gratitude came hard when one was trapped indoors with incompatible people. It was easy, now, to decide that I had imagined everything odd about Will. Homesickness had been the cause, no doubt. I was practical.

On Thursday, when Will and Scotty had been bickering over a game, Meg had suggested that I read to the boys. Surprised, I looked up from my book, a twice-read Nancy Drew mystery story.

Scotty looked skeptical, but Meg said, "Charlotte's really good at reading aloud. Give her a chance."

Scotty, scowling at the dust jacket on my book, said, "I don't want to hear a story about a girl."

Suddenly inspired, I said, "Then how about a story about a boy who finds a world where there are nine thousand dragons?"

Still skeptical, Scotty said, "What's it called?"

"*Nine Thousand Dragons*, of course," Meg said. "Will got it for Christmas—but we brought it along. Charlotte can read to you upstairs, in the bedroom."

The smile that Meg and Helen exchanged was not lost on me. So they were friends again? Who cared? I swallowed an angry retort and started for the stairs. They wanted to get rid of me as well as the boys, I decided. But I liked reading aloud, and I knew I was good. And it was an exciting book, worth reading once more. "Come on," I said to the boys, and they followed me reluctantly up to the attic.

The attic was not heated. What little warmth reached the rooms there came up the stairs, so the place was damp and uncomfortable. After I found the book, I tucked both boys into the double bed I shared with Meg, wrapped myself in the bedspread from Will's cot, and settled myself so that I leaned back against the headboard.

"'Chapter One, We Reach the Island,'" I began.

"Is this a true story?" Scotty interrupted sternly. "True stories are boring."

"Of course this isn't true," I said. "Dragons aren't real. They never were. Somebody made this up, so you don't have to be scared."

"I *wasn't* scared," Scotty explained with a great show of patience.

I began again, and both boys watched me as I read about the orphaned children cast adrift at sea after a storm, only to reach an island inhabited by dragons. But Scotty, much like a puppy, fell asleep within half an hour. Will, however, listened to every familiar word, his black eyes fixed on my face in a way that was almost unnerving.

I stopped reading. "Do you think I should go on? Scotty's missing the story."

"It won't make any difference to him," Will said. "You can begin in the middle of a story and he doesn't care. He just makes up the parts he doesn't hear."

"Have you been reading to him?" I asked, surprised.

Will shrugged. "Well, not stories. I read to him from the magazines. You know, stuff about Africa and South America and Canada."

I hesitated, then asked, "Are you talking about the magazines with the bookmarks?"

Will shrugged and looked away toward the window where rain ran down the panes. "Yeah."

"Do all those countries interest you?"

Will slid down in the bed so that his head rested on a pillow. "Not really," he said casually. "It gives Scotty something to think about. Otherwise, he worries that his mother might die."

"He does?"

"So do I," Will said quietly. "My mother, I mean."

"Nobody is going to die," I said firmly. "Now let's get back to the book." But a few minutes later I glanced up from a page and saw that Will, too, was fast asleep.

And the cat had reappeared and was sitting at the foot of the bed. I had not realized before this summer that a cat could wear an exasperated expression.

"Don't go to the woods," the cat said. "Don't read about them, either. Nothing in the magazines has anything to do with you. It's none of your business."

I stared.

"And that book *is* a true story," the cat said. "All books tell true stories. What's wrong with you that you didn't know that?"

I threw the book at him, missed, and the cat shot out the door. Both boys awoke, startled, crying, "What? What?"

I tossed off the bedspread and said, "Let's go down to the kitchen and see if Miss Warder will fix us some hot chocolate."

I picked up the book as I passed it and put it on the dresser I shared with Meg. The boys shoved past me and clattered down the stairs, having forgotten everything but the prospect of a treat. I watched for the cat as I made my way to the kitchen, but I did not see him.

Because he was never there, I told myself. I had been napping, too, just like the boys, and dreamed it.

After all, had I not always wanted to believe that all books are true?

Miss Warder produced not only hot chocolate but homemade doughnuts sprinkled with powdered sugar, and the other girls joined us in the breakfast room. To everyone's surprise, Jonah came in, too, scraping his chair up to the table and grabbing both of the remaining doughnuts with one hand.

"Your hair is wet," Helen commented critically. She had given up flirting with him and now seemed to despise him thoroughly.

"I was outside in the garden," he said, with his mouth full. "The pea vines in the garden were falling down in the rain, so I tied them up." He looked straight at me and said, "I walked down to the beach, too. There's a family of orcas playing in the water so close that I could see their markings. Too bad you missed it."

I would have loved seeing the family of killer whales playing, but I was not about to let Jonah know, so I pretended to shudder and said, "It's too cold outside."

"They don't mind the cold," Jonah said. He gulped down his hot chocolate and pushed himself away from the table. "That was good." Then he left as suddenly as he arrived.

I glanced at the boys and saw admiration on Scotty's face as he watched Jonah leave. It was not hard to read his mind. He wanted to be exactly like Jonah, a rude and exasperating boy who followed no rules. But the expression on Will's face was guarded. I thought that he did not envy Jonah as much as—what? Want to avoid him? I could not decide, and I was on the verge of asking Will what he was thinking when I felt something like a finger pressed to my lips. Stunned, I leaned back and the feeling went away, but it distracted me enough so that I did not ask the question. Will glanced at me, as if he had been aware of what had just happened, and then he looked away uneasily.

On Thursday, the rain let up for a while, and Jonah asked the Warders if Will could go with him for a bike ride. Miss Warder objected, but her brother said, "What a wonderful idea! Be sure to show him that back road behind the dairy farm. He'll like that. And the trail south of the beach."

"It's cold outside," I protested. I did not want Will going anywhere with weird Jonah, and I was sure that Miss Warder shared my apprehension, but Mr. Warder grabbed Will's jacket off the hook by the back door and held it out for him.

"Jonah, bring him back if the rain starts up again," Mr. Warder said, but all Jonah did was nod. He already had the back door open. Will hurried out, the door slammed, and I felt my skin prickle.

"Is Jonah . . . trustworthy?" I asked hesitantly.

Miss Warder, busy at the sink, said, "Of course he is. But . . ." Her voice trailed away.

"But what?" I asked.

Miss Warder turned on the water and rinsed a bowl. "But nothing," she said, and she laughed a little. "I'm sure Jonah will bring him back if it starts to rain again."

I left the kitchen, unsatisfied. I declined Mr. Warder's offer to ride into town for the papers and the mail, and I wandered into the sitting room. Scotty, as usual, was hunched over an atlas.

"What are you looking at this time?" I asked, not truly interested. I pulled an old novel from a shelf and sat down with it, turning the yellowed pages without reading a word.

"I'm trying to find where we are," Scotty said, peering closely at a page.

I got up to help him. He had the atlas open at the right page, but the map of Washington State did not include many details. I traced the edges of the southern and western edges of Puget Sound and could not be certain of where we were. "Maps don't show everything," I told Scotty.

"I like it better when I can see where something real is," Scotty said as he closed the atlas. "Will showed me where Seattle is, and I could put my finger on it. That's where my mom and dad are. And he showed me a place in another country where the Sky Wings go in winter. But he couldn't find Gull Walk."

He was about to get up and walk away when I grabbed his arm. "What Sky Wings?" I asked.

Scotty shrugged and pulled loose. "I don't know. Some kind of birds, I guess. Or maybe bugs, like those spirit things."

I let him go. I realized that I was holding my breath. I would have to talk to Will. He shouldn't be telling Scotty fairy tales that the little boy might end up believing. Sky

Wings and spirit *bugs*. Scotty was too young to be trusted to keep a secret. If there was a secret that had to be kept. Sometimes I thought that Will and I were sharing some sort of daydream.

A letter from Dad finally arrived that day, addressed to Meg, Will, and me. He enclosed a snapshot of the Navy officers' barracks where he lived, and another of him standing on a beach. "Maybe we'll all be together here in a house," he wrote. "Or maybe we'll all be together back home in Seattle." He sounded so confident that I could not help but feel better.

Better, even though Will had come back from his bike ride with muddy shoes and pants, and a strange look on his face. Better, even though I could not decide if he looked frightened or ecstatic. And he would not explain.

"Jonah and I went a long way," he said, shrugging in an elaborate attempt to seem casual.

But no one got muddy to the belt line riding a bike on wet roads, I thought. And later, when I went up to their bedroom, I found Will lying on his cot, and I suspected that he had been crying. But when I asked him, he denied it and said, "I was thinking about my parents—and missing them a lot."

I walked over to the window and looked down into the backyard. Jonah stood there, looking up at me. He was not smiling, but I could not judge his expression for certain. It was almost as if he pitied me.

Or was concerned for me.

Chapter 6

"He looked at the reflection in the pond, and he saw his true self," the Fox Fairy told the assembled creatures. "He saw that he was the Prince."

The Old Midwife tree sat still for a long moment. Then she rustled her branches irritably and said, "You, Griffin! Did you see this, too?"

The Griffin nodded. "I did, but when he saw his reflection in the water, he said, 'Who is that?' He was frightened, even after Fox tried to reassure him."

"They just stood there like great clods!" the Unicorn, said scornfully. "He needed comfort. He needed sympathy, while he grew accustomed to the truth."

The Griffin shook himself, snapped his beak angrily, and said, "We told him that he was the Prince. What more did he need?"

"Sympathy!" cried the Unicorn. "Consolation! Who would want to be the Prince? Who would want such a responsibility?"

"He didn't—and doesn't—know one single thing

about the responsibility involved," the Fox Fairy said. "Do you think we are mad? We only wanted him to know that he was born here, as the child of our lost leaders, and all things would be better for us and for him when he was ready to join us."

"And he burst into tears and tried to run away!" the Unicorn cried. "If my daughter had not been there, we would have lost him forever. She blocked his path and he stopped. He was not afraid of her."

"Well, who would be?" the Old Midwife asked disgustedly. "A baby unicorn with a horn the size of a Mudwalker's toe. I suppose she blabbed all of our secrets."

"She did not! She asked him if he wanted to see where the Spirit Lights live, and since he knows them and isn't afraid of them, he walked along with her and she showed him the nests. Afterward, he returned with her and looked into the pond again. And that time he almost seemed to accept what he saw, a Fair Prince."

"Ah," the Old Midwife said, satisfied. "Then who went back with him to the Guardians?"

"I did, of course," the Fox Fairy said. "He did not say much. But we need to be careful of the Between. I have seen into her future. She will try to run away with him, to keep him from us."

The Phoenix, who had been silent before, drew closer and said, "We trust your visions. But where would she take him? I thought you said that the young ones have no other home now."

"Not for a while," the Fox Fairy said. "Perhaps not until next summer. But she is a strong and determined Mudwalker. She might take all that she can perceive of us and act on it to keep the Prince from us. She won't want to lose him."

There was a long silence then before the Phoenix spoke again. "Then the Mudwalkers share some of our traits."

"Ha!" the Old Midwife cried. "Determination is the only one!"

"The Betweens are always different from the rest of them," the Fox Fairy said. "I might be able to explain to her. Perhaps. Later on. There is time, I hope. I only wish that the old Mudwalkers who stay with the Guardians would keep away forever. They are dangerous. I know it."

The Phoenix bent his head for a moment and then raised it again and said softly, "I will drive them out."

"Not you!" the Wyvern bellowed, pushing his way forward, his teeth flashing, his scales standing on end along his spine. He lashed his pointed tail and said, "I am the one who will drive them out! The sight of me will terrify them."

"I think we might be making a mistake if we try to frighten them away," the Fox Fairy said. "This could be work for the Pooka."

"What?" shouted the Old Midwife. "That fool? This isn't a time for jokes and tricks and aggravations."

"It might be," the Griffin said thoughtfully. "We could

begin with the Pooka's work—he can be very irritating— and if that does not succeed . . ."

"It will work!" the Pooka said. He pushed his way rudely into the center of the circle, tossing his goatlike head, thumping his big feet, and startling Spirit Lights out of the grass. "I will call on the Mudwalkers at night, when they sleep, and give them dreams that terrify them. I will destroy their belongings. I will turn their food to muck and their drink to poison."

"And if that doesn't work," said the Fox Fairy, "we can summon the Kelpie."

There was a long moment of respectful silence. Calling the Kelpie from the ocean was a serious matter. Messages would have to be carried by the Sky Wings across the forest and far out to sea. But she would come. She would have come during the Invasion of the Mudwalkers, if only there had been time to call her. But the attack had come so fast, so unexpectedly, and the Darkwood inhabitants had been so weak after the long winter and the logging, that there had been no time to send a message to the Kelpie, the seal woman who knew their history even better than the Old Midwife. Some of them, the Wyvern especially, believed that the Kelpie was the Creator, but who could prove that? The beginnings of history were too remote. And the Chimeras, who were the ones who said that, had been liars, one generation after another.

As if reading one another's minds, the Old Midwife

and the Phoenix said at the same time, "We were right to destroy the Chimera who lived here. We were right to drive him out of the woods so long that he weakened and died."

"If only there were a way to let the others know," the Fox Fairy said. "With all of the Chimeras destroyed, then perhaps all the other Darkwoods would be safe."

"Too late now," the young Dragon muttered from deep in the pond. "The Mudwalkers already exist, and they are everywhere. Now end this meeting. I am tired and I need to rest, if the Prince is coming. He will need me."

FROM CHARLOTTE THACKER'S NOTEBOOK

Will had come down with a cold, and I blamed that on his outing with Jonah. He spent the next two days in bed, restless and coughing. A great storm raged around Gull Walk one morning, slashing the windows with cold rain and tearing branches from the trees. Mr. Warder built a fire for us in the sitting room, but I worried about Will too much to be comfortable in the warm room, so I spent most of the afternoon in our attic bedroom, reading to him.

He did not want to hear the end of *Nine Thousand Dragons*, since he had read the book many times, but instead he asked me to read aloud some of the magazine articles about exotic jungles in tropical lands. I found the articles more boring than anything I had ever read, but Will seemed fascinated.

"Think of that," he said once. "Jungles that no one has ever seen. Hidden places where animals live who are always safe from people."

"That would be nice," I said. I looked down at him, lying with his eyes closed. His lashes seemed longer than ever, his face more pointed, his hair more of a silver color. His skin was so pale and delicate!

"Maybe I should ask Miss Warder to call a doctor for you," I said. "You don't look as if you're getting any better."

His eyes opened suddenly, and for a moment I thought I saw something there, something revealed that was wonderful and frightening and almost unimaginable.

"I'm better, honestly," he said. "I want to get up later today. I don't need a doctor."

"One more day in bed, just to be sure," I told him, and I picked up the magazine again.

"I think I'd rather sleep for a while," he said, yawning.

I closed the magazine and put it on the dresser. "See? You really are tired. Okay, I'll come up and check on you in a while."

I closed the door behind me and started down the stairs to the second floor, when I heard the harsh voice of Mrs. Fletcher echoing from below. "What difference does it make if we came back early! You'd think the hotel was full and we were inconveniencing somebody!"

Mr. Fletcher's voice rumbled something that I could not make out except for the word "necessary."

I was sorry they had come back a day early—such unpleasant people!—but there was nothing I could do about it. I passed the second floor and hurried down to the kitchen, where Miss Warder was beginning dinner preparations.

"Do you need help?" I asked.

Miss Warder flinched with surprise. "Heavens, Charlotte, but you startled me! The Fletchers are back, so I could use a little help, if you don't mind peeling vegetables. Your sister and Meg set the tables, and Scotty helped Jonah bring in firewood for the sitting room. Awful weather for June."

Then, surprising us both, we heard the bell ring from the counter near the front door.

"A new customer?" I asked.

Miss Warder shrugged, and wiping her hands dry on her apron, hurried from the room. I followed, curious. A couple with a teenage boy and a small girl stood in front of the counter. Miss Warder slipped behind it and asked, "Do you want rooms?"

"For one night," the man said. "Two rooms, and a cot in one of them for Maysie," he said, indicating the little girl.

"Certainly," Miss Warder said. "Do you mind sharing a connecting bath?"

"Perfect," the woman said. "That way I can keep an eye on everybody." She laughed, and Miss Warder laughed, too, a little nervously.

The man signed the big registration book, and Miss Warder handed him two keys. Then, seeing me watching, she said, "Will you help them with their bags, Charlotte?"

But the man waved her off, saying, "We don't have much, and Ted and I can manage it."

Miss Warder introduced me to the Hardings, and Mrs. Harding told me the names of her children, Ted and Maysie. I nodded, feeling stupid and unneeded. The rooms they had been given were at the opposite end of the second floor from the Fletchers' room, and the bathroom the family would share was the one I had used, more than once. Someone had cleaned it each time, probably Mr. Warder, but I could not be sure that he had done it that morning. There was not time for me to run upstairs and check the bathroom now.

I hurried into the sitting room and found my sister and Helen playing dominos at the card table, and Scotty looking through Will's stack of comic books. "New people have checked in," I told them. "And the awful Fletchers are back."

The girls stared in disbelief, but Scotty did not look up. "The Fletchers are back already?" Meg said. "I can't stand them. I wish they had stayed away forever."

"Who are the new people?" Helen asked. "Do they have a girl our age?"

"Their name is Harding, and their little girl looks about four years old," I said. "But they have a boy named Ted, and he's probably your age."

"Oh, good," Helen said, pushing back her chair. "Let's meet them."

"They're going upstairs now," I said, with a certain satisfaction in disappointing Helen. Ted was nice looking, with dark curly hair and big brown eyes. Maybe Meg would be interested in him and forget about the treacherous Angus.

"They'll be down for dinner, I suppose," Meg said, stacking the dominos back in the box and sighing. Clearly, Angus was still on her mind.

"Yes, and we'll be sitting in the little side room, out of sight and out of mind," Helen said. "Come on, Scotty, let's go up the front stairs and see if we can run into them, accidentally on purpose."

"Let's all go," I said, tugging at Meg's sleeve. Any change could be a good one, in a remote place like Gull Walk.

But we reached the second floor in time to hear the Hardings' doors close just as the Fletchers' door opened. The elderly couple approached us, scowling.

"Are you allowed to use the guests' stairs?" Mrs. Fletcher asked. Her hard eyes flickered over us, and without waiting for an answer to her first question, she asked, "Where's that spindly little kid?"

Spindly! I opened my mouth to protest, but Meg spoke first.

"Our brother has a cold, so he's in bed," she said. Her tone did not invite another comment from Mrs. Fletcher.

But the ugly woman did not take Meg's cool voice as a warning. "Is he really your brother?" she asked. "He doesn't look anything like you girls. And he's so sickly. Are you sure all he has is a cold? Miss Warder said that you had to stay here because your mother is in a hospital somewhere. What's wrong with her?"

I was stunned. I would have pushed past the woman and run upstairs, but Meg grabbed my arm so hard that it hurt. "We're spending our summer vacation here," Meg said loudly. "With our cousins."

"My father is related to the Warders," Helen added, with her very best smirk. "We come here often, and this time we brought our cousins. Aren't we lucky?"

Helen's comment seemed to annoy Mrs. Fletcher, and she walked away without waiting for her husband. I was pleased to see that both her stockings had runs and the hem of her skirt had come down in back. Mr. Fletcher followed clumsily, nearly stumbling over the carpet. He did not look back.

"So much for them," Helen said. "I loathe them. They're always snooping around."

"Snooping? What do you mean?" I asked, surprised and uneasy.

"Snooping!" Helen repeated irritably. "You know, poking around where you don't belong. Once I caught her outside our bedroom door. She told me she had gotten confused about the floors, as if anyone would believe that. Another time she was watching Scotty and Will playing outside and I didn't like how she stared at them. Well, at Will, particularly. As if he was a bug or something."

"What?" Meg asked.

"Well, she had a funny look on her face, as if she didn't like him."

"She doesn't even know him!" I protested.

"And she's not going to," Meg said firmly. "What an awful woman!"

We went to our room silently. The newest guests did not seem important now. I wondered if Mrs. Fletcher had ever seen Will without his shadow. Or playing with the ball of sparks. That could be dangerous for my brother.

Will had his dinner on a tray in his room, but the rest of us ate in the breakfast room, very aware of the new guests in the hotel. It would have been hard to ignore them, I thought as I picked at my food. The Fletchers were bombarding the Hardings with questions: Where had they come from? How long were they staying? Had they ever been in this part of Washington before? Where were they going next? They carried on as if they thought the Hardings were Nazi spies.

The Hardings clearly were annoyed, and I suspected that they left their table before finishing their dessert. A few minutes later, the four of them went away in their car. I saw it through the windows, heading toward town.

"They're probably looking for another place to stay," I said loudly, hoping that the Fletchers heard me. "Who wants to be asked so many questions?"

"The Fletchers do ask a lot about things," Scotty said. "All the time."

Helen looked down at him, frowning. "They ask *you* questions? What kind?"

"Oh, about Will and Charlotte and Meg," he said. "How long they're going to stay and things like that."

I saw Meg bite her lip. "What did you tell them?" she asked.

Scotty shrugged. "I said they were staying as long as we stayed, which would be until our new baby was big and strong, and Mama could take care of all of us again."

I let out the breath I had been holding. The answer should put an end to the Fletchers' curiosity. And it cut off any curiosity they might have about Mother, I hoped. There was no need for strangers to know about her illness. Miss Warder was kind and friendly, and probably she did not think of how her information might sound to strangers.

Or perhaps Mrs. Fletcher had nagged it out of her.

Jonah came late to lunch, as usual, and offered no apology. He only picked at his main dish, but he bolted down his dessert and then announced that he was going upstairs to visit Will.

"Leave him alone!" I blurted.

Everyone stared at me, astonished.

"He's probably sleeping," I said in a more reasonable tone.

"He's eating his meal on a tray!" Meg argued. "He'd probably love some company."

Jonah did not wait for the argument to conclude, but ran off, and I heard him going up the bare back stairs. I did not like the idea of Jonah talking to Will alone. There was more to Jonah than was obvious. He was sneaky and probably a liar—and perhaps something else.

And what was he doing in the woods that day?

In the big dining room, the Fletchers began complaining loudly about their food and Miss Warder came running.

"It tastes terrible!" Mrs. Fletcher cried. "I won't eat another bite of it. You'll have to bring us something else."

"But what's wrong with it?" Miss Warder asked.

"Everything!" Mr. Fletcher said. "Half is burned and the rest is still raw!"

"Maybe you just don't want to take the time to cook

well," Mrs. Fletcher told Miss Warder. "Maybe you're taking us for granted now because we've come here so much."

"I think everything tastes fine," Meg said, loud enough to be heard clear out on the road.

"So do I," Helen added. "We've eaten every last bite of it."

"Bring us something different, right now," Mrs. Fletcher said. Her voice crackled with anger. "And bring fresh water. This is no better than ditch water."

"Are they crazy?" Meg asked.

"Yes," Helen snickered. "We already knew that."

When we finished eating, we cleared the table and carried the dishes out to the kitchen. Miss Warder had cut thick slices of ham and was making an omelette with tomatoes and peppers for the Fletchers. She seemed ready to cry, and her eyes were red-rimmed.

"Don't mind them," Helen told her. "They're just being nasty for the fun of it. Probably they were thrown out of the place they were staying in Portland."

Miss Warder smiled a little, but she shook her head. "They're regular customers. We don't want to start talk about us. Even if . . ."

"If what?" Meg asked.

Miss Warder only shook her head again. "They don't fit in, exactly, if you know what I mean."

"They're creepy," Scotty said. "That's what I think."

"That's enough," Helen said, and she took him away

by the hand. "Let's play dominos again."

"Said she, as she leaves us to clean up the kitchen," Meg said, laughing.

"That's all right," I said. "I'd rather keep busy."

Miss Warder, silent and frowning a little, carried the new dinner plates in to the Fletchers, and we started in on the dishes. "Someday somebody will invent a machine to do this and everybody will have one," I said.

"Don't you wish?" Meg said as she rinsed a plate. "Did you ever notice that Mr. Warder doesn't hang around much when the Fletchers are here?"

I shrugged. "He's always around somewhere, though, just not in the same room with them. But he waits on them sometimes."

"But mostly he doesn't. I think he doesn't like them any better than we do."

"But he doesn't seem to care if Gull Walk stays open or not," I said. "The Fletchers are regular customers, and I guess they're better than nothing."

Meg sloshed more soap into the hot water. "Mr. Warder will like the Hardings," she said confidently.

"So you *did* notice them," I said.

"Why not?" Meg answered. "We'll be here forever, probably, and I'll bet Angus has already asked Bibi to go steady. He never asked me."

"What do you care?" I said, wiping a dish dry. "He has jug ears."

Meg laughed reluctantly and I felt rewarded.

And then I looked out the window and saw Jonah pushing his bike out toward the road. "We forgot Will's tray," I told Meg, doing my best to hide my panic. "I'll run up and get it."

I flew up the back stairs, one flight and then two, and opened the door to the room I shared with my brother.

The tray lay on the top of the dresser, and Will stared up at me in surprise. The covers were pulled to his chin.

But his innocent act did not fool me. I yanked the covers back and saw that he was completely dressed, just as I had suspected.

"Where do you think you're going?" I cried.

"Nowhere," he lied. His long-lashed black eyes looked back at me without blinking.

"Were you going to meet Jonah somewhere?" I asked, not sure where the question came from, but knowing that it was the right one to ask.

Now Will blinked. "No," he said.

"Liar," I said. "You were going after him with Mr. Warder's bike, weren't you?"

Silence.

"You're still sick," I said. "Do you want to end up in a hospital, like Mama? It could happen, if you're not careful."

Will sighed. "I'll get back into my pajamas. Don't make such a fuss about everything."

I turned my back while he changed, and after I tucked him back into bed, I warned him once more about staying there, and then I carried his tray down to the kitchen. I did not tell Meg about what I had seen, because one thing could lead to another, one question to another. There was still the chance that bossy Meg might write to Dad and create problems. If the Thacker family needed anything, it was not more problems than we already had.

But early in the evening, I told Miss Warder that I needed to walk for a while—I had been shut up inside too long—and I left Gull Walk, heading toward the road that ran by the fenced woods. I could not help but be curious, even though I was afraid. There was Jonah's bike again. Wasn't that a gate in the fence? I had not seen it before. But when I reached the place, I saw that it was not a gate after all. Had I only imagined it?

I walked closer to the fence, and finally, cautiously, I climbed over, doing my best to avoid the cruel barbs. Ahead of me somewhere, Jonah was walking. Or hiding. Or up to something that he wanted my brother to be part of. Perhaps it was time to have it out with him, here where we could not be overheard. Where he could tell the truth, if the truth was even in him.

A flare of sparks flew up before me, nearly blinding me. I stepped back, raising my hands to protect my eyes. And then I saw that they were not sparks, but small winged creatures.

"Stay out of the woods," they cried. "Stay out! Stay out! Stay out! We don't want you here."

I stumbled away and climbed the fence, snagging my skirt on the top wire. I heard myself crying, but it seemed as if it were someone else, someone much younger, someone who believed in fairies.

And monsters.

The sky was leaden and heavy with rain, hanging low over the world. As I ran, I could smell salt water and fir trees. And something else, something strange and pungent. I saw a large, longhaired goat in the field beside the road. It trotted along the ditch, parallel to the road, watching me with strange, glowing eyes. Once it reared up, pawing the air. I ran faster. It was so big! Too big for a goat.

And then it was gone. A scrawny rabbit bounded through the grass, and it, too, watched me. "Run, Charlotte," it said. "Don't go back to the woods. The woods are not for you."

I cried aloud, terrified. I had a stitch in my side, and my lungs hurt. Gull Walk seemed too far away to reach safely. Were there footsteps in the road behind me? I was afraid to look. And then, in the distance, where the field sloped down to the shore, I saw a horse galloping, tossing his head. And then it was a goat. And then it was a rabbit bounding high above the grass.

And then footsteps pursued me again.

"Stay out of the woods," something said.

❖ ❖ ❖

At Gull Walk, I told Meg that I was coming down with Will's cold and thought I would go to bed early. Meg, playing checkers with Helen in the breakfast room, accepted my excuse with little interest, and I was grateful. Who would believe what had happened to me that day? Who could I tell? And who would help me, if Will was somehow involved with all this?

When I reached our room, I was not surprised to see that Will's cot was empty. I shoved open the window and leaned out. Below, in the chilly early evening, he was pushing Mr. Warder's bike around the corner of Gull Walk, toward the road that led to the woods. Sparks circled his head and streamed ahead of him, leading the way.

"Charlotte, stay out of the woods," the cat said from the roof above my head. "Ask no questions. What is being done now must be done, for you as well as us."

"Leave me alone!" I cried. "Will!" I shouted after my brother, but my voice was swept away in a sudden gust of wind.

Shaking, I lay down on my bed and pulled the quilt over my head.

Chapter 7

"He grows more comfortable with us," the Fox Fairy said. "But he is still attached to the Mudwalkers. Too attached."

The Griffin, grooming himself, said, "He has been with them for years. This will take time."

"Time! We don't have time. The Mudwalkers are everywhere." The Midwife threw twigs fretfully. "Mudwalkers cut down trees, Mudwalkers kill animals, and the Mudwalker wars will destroy the entire world, their own and ours, too. We must hide from them, especially now that the Prince is here. When he grows strong and older, then we will have less to fear from them."

The Griffin stopped grooming long enough to say, "The noble Fair Ones could not save us before. They were the first to die. We must not put all our faith in their child. We need to plan carefully."

"We need to find a way to join our Darkwoods with the others," the Phoenix said. "If we had corridors connecting us, corridors of forest linking us all over the world, then perhaps we could take back what was ours."

"There is no way," the Old Midwife said. "It's too late. There are too many Mudwalkers. There is no hope any-where, not even with the Prince nearby."

"When he is grown, he will be wise, and he will show us a way," the Fox Fairy said. "To believe anything else will cause us more harm than the Mudwalkers ever could."

"Spare me another lecture on courage," the Old Midwife said. The unicorn colt was butting at her trunk again, and she smacked the brat with a low-hanging branch. The colt ran to her mother, squeaking.

"Stop squabbling," the Dragon grumbled from beneath the pond. "The Prince has come, he has seen his kingdom, and he will accept his future. That is all you can hope for now. But if you waste your strength in arguing, then you neglect his safety. If something hap-pens to him, this Darkwood will be lost, too. And the Chimera will have won the world." He growled some-thing unintelligible, and the surface of the pond rippled. The others knew that he was almost ready to hatch, almost ready to rise to the surface. And when he did, that part of the world would be changed. The final battle would begin.

From Charlotte Thacker's notebook

Will sneaked back in bed only moments before Meg climbed the stairs at ten o'clock that night. He avoided looking at me and, still dressed, slid under his blankets. With a deep sigh, he turned his face to the wall and closed his eyes.

When Meg opened the door, she whispered, "Is Will sleeping?"

I was tempted to tell my sister everything, but I angrily held my tongue. Meg would not believe me anyway. I almost hated my brother at that moment for putting me in this position.

"He's probably worn out," I said as I sat up. "Don't worry about waking him."

"What did you think of Ted Harding?" Meg asked. "He seemed nice, and he paid as much attention to me as he did to Helen."

I was not interested in whether or not Ted Harding paid attention to anyone. "They're leaving in the morning," I said. "So it doesn't matter what I think."

"Did you notice that man who checked in after dinner?" Meg asked as she pulled her nightgown over her head and undressed under it.

"What man?" I asked. "Where did you see him?"

"In the hall, by the reception desk. I heard him tell Mr.

Warder he was a friend of the Fletchers and wanted a room near them."

"As if the Fletchers had a friend anywhere on the face of the earth," I scoffed, but at the same time I was worried. If he was as curious about Will as they were, things could only get harder for us.

"He's awfully ugly," Meg said. "I know we aren't supposed to say things like that, but he really is. He's stout—sort of bulky and awkward—and he has thick fingers. He jabs them in the air when he talks. I don't think Mr. Warder liked him at all."

"But it would be nice if Gull Walk was full for the summer," I said, just for the sake of saying something. I was no longer certain that having lots of people around was a good idea. "I worry more than the Warders about the place closing."

Meg put her folded clothes on the chair in the corner and crawled between the sheets. "Whatever happens will happen, I guess."

The window was open a few inches, and I could smell salt water and evergreen trees. This could have been such a peaceful, ordinary place.

I rolled over on my stomach and buried my face in my pillow. Everything I had seen that concerned Will, everything I had heard, was impossible. And, even worse, it was crazy.

I flopped over on my back with a sigh. Meg, fussing with the top sheet, smoothing the top hem carefully over the edge of the blanket the way she always did, looked across at me. "Are you going to have another of those nights when you toss and mutter for hours? I don't think I can stand it."

"Did you ever have something like a dream, only when you were awake?" I asked quietly. I was taking a big chance.

"Certainly," Meg answered crisply. "I dreamed that Angus would ask me to be his steady girlfriend and even marry me someday." She yanked the covers up to her chin. "Fat lot of good that did me."

"I don't mean that kind of dream," I said. "I don't mean wishful thinking."

"Then what are you talking about?"

"I mean, did you ever imagine that an animal was trying to talk to you?" I whispered as I raised up on one elbow. Will did not move. I could not tell if he was listening.

Meg giggled. "You sound like Will. He's always said that animals could talk. Don't you remember when he first came to live with us, and he used to talk to the dogs in the neighborhood? He said they answered back."

"He was practically a baby," I said. "Little kids imagine all sorts of things." Oh, let that be the truth, I thought.

"Well, I don't imagine talking animals," Meg said. "Go to sleep."

But I lay awake for a long time, and after a while the cat jumped to the windowsill and said, "Don't worry.

Don't be afraid. Everything is happening the way it should happen."

I covered my ears. Meg was sleeping, but had Will heard the cat? He did not stir.

The practical path would be to stop Will from having anything more to do with Jonah, and that could be accomplished best by telling the Warders that Jonah took Will out for long bike rides when he was not well enough. The Warders, especially Miss Warder, would worry about Will's health and put a stop to Jonah's sneaking around. Probably. But Will was not going to have a cold forever. A long summer stretched ahead of us. Whatever strange magic had entangled Will could grow much worse, and Jonah might not be the source of it. There was the cat, too.

I needed advice, but where would I get it? From Meg? The thought made me almost laugh aloud. I could not write to Dad and worry him. The Warders would not believe what I told them because Gull Walk was their home, and surely they had never seen anything like the balls of sparks and the talking cat. They might become offended. They had no reason to keep the Thacker children for the summer, since we were not related. Where might we be sent, if the Warders wanted us gone from Gull Walk?

In the morning, the Hardings left immediately after breakfast, a meal that was spoiled for everyone by the loud complaints from the Fletchers, who once again found their food inedible. They had not been able to sleep, either, they declared, because their bed was lumpy and they thought they had heard rats—or animals of some kind—running around in the walls. And they were certain that somebody had been going through their drawers, because the clothing had been left mussed up and untidy. I wondered if Mrs. Fletcher was blaming us.

I was clearing our breakfast table, and I heard Miss Warder tell her brother that she wished they would just leave.

"Oh yes," he said. "Indeed. That would be best. But we still need to bring in enough money to pay the property taxes." He sounded so serious that I looked through the kitchen door at him and caught his expression of deep concern before he changed it when he saw me watching. "Well, we're always sorry when we don't please people, Charlotte," he said.

"But I thought the Fletchers have been coming here for years," I said. "The food is very good—and I didn't hear anything moving around in the walls. Maybe there's something wrong with *them.*" I wanted to add that none of us had been going through their drawers, either, if that was what they had been implying, because we knew better. But I was not sure if Jonah knew better or not.

"Ah, what a loyal girl," Mr. Warder said, laughing.

"You are quite right. There is something wrong with them."

"And there has been, ever since we bought the woods," Miss Warder muttered.

"What?" I asked. "*You* own the woods?"

"It was one way to keep hunters out," Mr. Warder said easily. "We fenced it and posted it with 'No Hunting' signs."

"So no one is supposed to go there?" I asked. Will must stay away, then!

"There's no reason to go there," Miss Warder said. "No reason at all. There's nothing to see. That's the way the animals like it. No changes and no people."

"I don't blame them," I said quietly. I would speak to Will—and Jonah, too. He must not take Will into the woods again.

The friend of the Fletchers, Mr. Blade, had sat at their table at breakfast, and they had made a great show of delight in his company—and also a great show of apologizing for the terrible food. After eating, they dawdled over their coffee, and I, willing to believe anything bad about them then, thought that they did this deliberately to delay Miss Warder from clearing up the last of the breakfast dishes.

Shamelessly eavesdropping from the stair landing, I decided that the Fletchers had asked this man to come, for some specific reason.

Mr. Blade was taller than Mr. Fletcher, and husky,

as if he was accustomed to hard labor. His suit seemed too small for him. His gray hair was cut short and his nose was too big for his face. His mouth turned down, as if smiling were a strange expression for him. He was a frightening man.

I hurried quietly up the stairs to my room. Meg had borrowed an iron and ironing board from Miss Warder and she was pressing our freshly washed clothes. The room smelled of damp cotton and starch. Meg looked up when I came in and said, "What's wrong?"

"I hate that Mr. Blade."

"That's all right, because I hate everybody who comes here," Meg said. She concentrated on her ironing.

Will, lying on top of his cot and fully dressed, said, "What's wrong with Mr. Blade?"

"Well, first of all, he's a friend of the Fletchers, and they're trying to pretend that they're surprised that he's here."

"Why would they really want a friend of theirs to come here if they hate the food so much?" practical Meg asked. "I've been expecting them to leave."

"Well, he's here now, complaining about the food right along with them."

"Who cares?" Will said, yawning. He picked up the comic book he had been reading, but I watched him staring at one place on a single page and knew that he was not reading. What was he thinking? As soon as I had an opportunity to be alone with him, I would warn him about the woods.

Lunch was late because an animal of some kind had gotten into the kitchen and pulled the pan of fried chicken off the counter. Miss Warder had only caught a quick glimpse of it, she said, and it looked like a goat! A goat! I almost told them that I had seen one, but I was afraid of their asking questions.

"Nobody around here keeps goats," Mr. Warder said. "You must have seen a dog."

"With horns?" Miss Warder said. "Well, the chicken was spilled all over the floor, so what do I do now?"

"Serve it," I said from the doorway. I knew the Fletchers and Mr. Blade were waiting in the dining room, and the thought of them eating food that had been dropped on the floor pleased me enormously.

The Warders stared at me, then both began laughing. "Charlotte!" Miss Warder said. "We couldn't do that."

"I could—and I would. Your floor is clean, so I don't mind having chicken that fell on it. And the Fletchers and Mr. Blade don't deserve anything else."

The chicken was served. We ate ours, and even Jonah seemed to enjoy his food for once. The Fletchers, however, complained noisily about the chicken tasting like liver and Mrs. Fletcher added that if the food did not improve immediately, they would have to leave.

"Quiet," Mr. Blade said suddenly, sharply.

I heard him giving Mrs. Fletcher the order, and I

shivered. He was supposed to be their friend? I was even more suspicious of him then.

The sun came out after lunch, and the Fletchers and their friend left immediately in the Fletchers' car. They made a point of assuring the Warders that they would be eating dinner at a better place, and I could see that Miss Warder's patience was worn to a sliver by then.

As soon as the car left, the mood at Gull Walk improved. Meg and Helen washed their hair and sat on the back porch, drying in the sun. Scotty found a pile of old bricks at the edge of the garden and spent the afternoon building himself a fort.

Will spent most of the time in our room, coughing sometimes, reading comic books, or dozing. I looked in on him and told him he must not go to the woods again, because the Warders owned them and did not want people there.

Will was irritated by my concern. "Stop fussing over me," he complained.

"And stay away from Jonah," I added. "There's something wrong with him."

"There's nothing wrong with him!" Will shouted. "And I don't want to stay inside all the time."

"If you go anywhere again without telling me, I'll make sure Dad hears about it," I told him. "Maybe I'll even tell Mama the next time I write to her."

"You aren't supposed to write anything that will upset her," Will said.

"Then you'd better behave."

But he would do as he pleased, I knew.

After a peaceful dinner, Mr. Warden invited us to go with him to see double feature movies at the theater in town. Meg, Helen, and Scotty agreed immediately, but Will said that he did not feel well enough yet. I thought that Will should not go, either, but I did not believe his excuse. Miss Warder, however, offered the opinion that Will might catch something else if he sat in a crowded theater, so of course, he should stay at Gull Walk and go to bed early.

Will looked so satisfied with her comment that I was even more suspicious. "I'll stay here, too," I said.

"But you like movies," Will said. He was up to something. He was being much too agreeable about not going to the movies.

"I have a little bit of a headache," I said definitely. "I'll stay here."

Will scowled, but I only smiled benignly at him. You won't get away from me this time, I thought.

Mr. Warder drove away with the girls and Scotty before eight o'clock, and I, who had been following Will around from one place to another, still trailed after him as he climbed the stairs.

"Are you going to bed now?" I asked. "I think you should. We can read for a while, until it gets dark."

"Sure," Will said slowly, tiredly. "Sure."

It was too hot to get under the covers, so Will made himself comfortable on top of his cot and opened one of the magazines he loved. I gathered up my pajamas and toothbrush and hurried down the flight of stairs to the second floor staff bathroom. It would not take me more than four or five minutes, I thought. What could Will do in that time?

But when I got back, the room was empty. I looked out the window, and saw Will running out the back gate toward the garden—and the beach—and sparks circled his head like a halo and streamed behind him.

I dressed faster than I ever had before and shot down the stairs, but just as I reached the back door, Miss Warder grabbed her arm.

"The Fletchers are watching. You have to pretend that Will is still here."

"What?" I cried. I was stunned. What was Miss Warder talking about?

"They parked their car up the road, among some trees. I can see them from my bedroom window. You can't let them know he's gone. If you rush out shouting for him, they'll hear and know he's taken the beach path. They could catch him!"

"Catch him? Why? What do you mean?"

"They think they know who he is," Miss Warder said.

"Of course they know! He is Will Thacker, my brother."

Miss Warder looked straight into my eyes for a long

moment, and then she said, "They must not catch him alone."

My heart seemed to thud in my chest. "But that doesn't make any sense. Why would they *catch* him? Are you talking about kidnapping?"

This was so ridiculous! The Fletchers would not want to take Will away. They had not made any effort to hide their dislike of him.

Both of us heard a car come into the Gull Walk driveway, and we ran to see who was there. It was the Fletchers' car, and they were getting out of it—without their friend.

"Remember what I said," Miss Warder hissed in my ear. "They must not learn that Will is out of the house alone."

She was scaring me to death. I ran upstairs to the bedroom and looked out the window, hoping to catch a glimpse of Will. But he was gone. I thought I saw Jonah skulking up the beach path toward Gull Walk, but I could not be sure. I could not think of what to do. Nothing made sense.

Oh, why had Meg gone into town? I nearly cried aloud. If she were here, I would tell her everything, even if she didn't believe me.

The cat jumped to the windowsill and stepped inside the room. "Listen carefully," he said. "Your brother is safe for now, but the Mudwalkers must not learn where he is. Make them believe that he is here, with you. He needs time to learn the History. They must not catch him."

"What?" I gasped.

The cat sighed. "Your brother is not like you. He is not a Mudwalker. He only looks like one. Right now he is learning about his proper place. Help us keep him safe."

"Mudwalker?" I asked hoarsely. "What is that?"

"You," the cat said. "You are a Mudwalker. People are Mudwalkers, created as toys by a Chimera who has since paid for his sin. Your brother is hiding as a Mudwalker, and some of them know it. They are trying to catch him before he returns to Darkwood to save the real world. *The real world.*"

He leaped back to the windowsill and looked over his shoulder at me. "Don't let them discover that he is not here. I charge you with that."

And he was gone.

I slid to the floor and buried my face in my quilt. None of this is true, I told myself. None of it.

Someone knocked on my door. "Charlotte?" Miss Warder asked. "Charlotte, would you and Will like to come down for chocolate cake? The Fletchers brought it back with them." Her voice was strained. "I wasn't sure about Will—he didn't seem to feel well at all. But they've asked . . ."

I scrubbed tears off my face and got to my feet. It took me a moment to find the courage to open the door, and when I did, I saw that Miss Warder was so pale that she looked ill. "Please!" Miss Warder mouthed to me. "Say no."

I struggled to think of the right answer. "I'll come down," I said finally, loudly enough to be heard at least on the floor below. "But Will has a sore throat. Could I bring him a piece of cake so that he doesn't have to get up?"

"Oh, the poor boy," Miss Warder said, catching on instantly. She hurried down the stairs ahead of me, and I followed unsteadily, half expecting to simply faint and put an end to the entire nightmare.

The Fletchers were standing in the lower hall. He carried a bakery box and she wore a smile that chilled me more than an open threat.

"Where's the boy?" asked Mrs. Fletcher.

"He's in bed," I said. "He has such a sore throat that he can hardly swallow, but I'm sure he'd try to eat a small piece of cake."

"He should come down here," Mr. Fletcher boomed. "It must be hot and stuffy in that attic. Why don't I go up and ask him myself?"

For a moment, I panicked. Why did they want to know anything about my brother? Then I saw a clear way out of this. "Will isn't well at all, and we think he'll need to see the doctor tomorrow. You know what happened to our mother, don't you?"

The Fletchers stared at me.

"Our mother has tuberculosis," I said, raising my

voice. I was gathering my strength now, determined to put them off the idea of visiting Will. "She's in a sanatorium. Of course, we were all checked by the doctors, but they warned us that something might show up later. Something awful. And we have to be careful. So if Will has caught—umm—*something*—from Mama, then he needs to see a doctor and other people should stay away from him. Meg and I have already been exposed, but you haven't." I took a step forward, coughed, and said, "Sad, isn't it?"

The Fletchers took a step backward instantly.

"I'll cut a small piece of the cake and you can bring it up to him," Miss Warder said.

"I'll wait right here," I said. I smiled at the Fletchers. "I'm sure Miss Warder will bring plates and forks into the dining room for you so that you can enjoy your dessert. Why don't you wait in there and be comfortable—and safe?"

"Yes," Mrs. Fletcher said distantly, as if she had a great deal on her mind and was not certain what to do next.

"By the way," I went on, frightened by my own behavior, "what happened to your friend? Mr. Blade, is it? Yes, why didn't he come back with you?"

"I'm picking him up later," Mr. Fletcher said roughly. "He's spending a little time with friends." He took his wife by the arm and steered her toward the dining room.

I sat on the bottom step, feeling as if I were guarding a castle. Nothing that had happened in the last half hour made any sense to me. I'll wake up in a minute, I thought, and find out that this was all a dream. And I'll tell Meg about it while we're getting dressed.

Miss Warder came back with a small tray holding a slice of cake and a glass of water. "I hope you're hungry," she whispered. "You'll have to finish it."

"Thank you, Miss Warder," I said loudly.

I climbed the stairs quickly, afraid to look behind me. When I reached my room, I let myself inside quickly and closed the door. For the first time since I arrived at Gull Walk, I turned the key in the lock.

Now what?

I could not bear the idea of eating the cake, but I must, for sooner or later I would have to take the tray back down and if the Fletchers were around, they would need more proof that Will was in bed.

I smiled wryly. Tuberculosis was a disease that frightened people. It was like a plague. At one time, anyone who got it eventually died of it. Catching the disease meant a long, long hospitalization, as well as the danger of exposing family members and friends. For once—and once only—I was glad that Mama had tuberculosis rather than appendicitis, which would not frighten off anyone.

I ate the cake, but I had barely finished when someone knocked on the door.

"Yes?" I asked.

"How is Will?"

It was Mrs. Fletcher! I pressed my hands against my mouth. What was I supposed to do now? Say he was asleep? Even if he had been sleeping, he would have awakened by loud talking.

The cat slid in the open window. "I'm sick," he wailed in Will's voice.

There was a moment of silence outside the door.

"I wish you hadn't disturbed him," I said loudly. "He was almost asleep again."

The cat sobbed, just as Will would have sobbed. "My throat hurts," he cried.

"I just thought I'd look in on him for a second," Mrs. Fletcher said.

The cat coughed and wept.

"Please, Mrs. Fletcher, you're only upsetting him!" I said sharply. "We have enough trouble already."

"If you're sure . . ." Mrs. Fletcher said. Attempting to sound kind did not come easily to her.

"Go away," I said. "Will needs to rest. You wouldn't want to be responsible for anything bad happening to him. My father wouldn't like it. And you wouldn't want to come down with anything, would you?"

There was a pause, and then Mrs. Fletcher said, "I'll look in on him tomorrow. Just for a second or two."

Yes, and with a handkerchief held over your nose and mouth, I thought bitterly.

"All right," I said. "Good night."

The cat turned and was ready to leave when I stopped him with one word. "No!"

He looked back at me, apparently astonished at my tone.

"How can you talk like Will?" I demanded.

"The same way I can talk like Meg," he said in Meg's voice.

Tears spurted in my eyes. "I don't understand anything."

"And rightly so, because it's none of your business," the cat said. "Wipe your nose and stop blubbering, Four Eyes. In an hour or so, Will will be back again, in time to climb into bed and have a good night's sleep."

Four Eyes. The cat laughed and jumped off the windowsill and was gone.

A ladybug crawled along the edge of the window shade for an inch or two and then stopped. I watched, not knowing what to expect.

The ladybug turned solemnly in a circle, shook itself, and then changed into a slender winged creature. It cried something unintelligible and seemed to wait for an answer.

"I don't understand you," I whispered, terrified.

The creature shook itself again and then piped, "I . . . said . . . that . . . the . . . Fox . . . is . . . rude."

"Fox?" I asked. "Do you mean *cat*?"

The creature stared at me for a long moment, and

then said, "You . . . are . . . quite . . . stupid."

And it flew out the window into the night.

There were two people who knew what was going on. The Warders. I pushed my hair away from my face and left my bedroom. "No, no," something whispered to me, but I started down the stairs to the kitchen.

Chapter 8

"The ugly old Mudwalkers are still here," the Fox Fairy reported. "And a friend has joined them. He smells like a Chimera."

The Unicorn raised her head quickly. "Where could he have come from? We believed that most of them had been destroyed."

"We must be certain first that he is a Chimera," the Old Midwife said. "If we do anything that draws attention to us, they all will come here, all the Mudwalkers, and then what?"

"The Prince is the one who is most important," the Fox Fairy said.

"Most of the time he stands at the edge of the woods," the Old Midwife complained. "He has been with the Mudwalkers too long. Clearly, he does not want to be with us."

"Give him the opportunity to become accustomed to our appearance," the Unicorn said. "Some of us are beautiful, but others . . . well, the Wyvern is quite frightening."

"Too bad your daughter doesn't think so," the Wyvern complained. The scales growing along his spine rose up. "She has no respect for me or anyone else."

"Don't take your naps out in the open, then," the Unicorn said. "She was only playing, and she didn't hurt you."

"Are we going to talk about spoiled offspring or are we going to talk about our Prince?" the Fox Fairy said.

"Perhaps he is a spoiled offspring," the Phoenix said sadly. "Spoiled by his association with Mudwalkers. If the Prince is happy with them, why should he want to return to us, when all that would mean is training for battles—and then the battles themselves, if the worst happens."

"Battles if the Guardians die and the woods fall into the hands of others," the Griffin said. He sighed deeply. "We always knew it could come to that."

"But we hoped that our Prince would be returned to us and save us!" the Old Midwife cried.

"He is here by the merest chance," the Fox Fairy said. "If his Mudwalker mother had not fallen ill, we never would have seen him again."

"I remember the terrible day when his Fair mother sent him out to the road," the Old Midwife wept. "She was dying . . . the king had already died . . . and she turned her child toward the road and said, 'You are Mudwalker now! Go to the road and wait for one of them to pick you up. That is the only way you can stay alive.' And he went."

"I took him," the Fox Fairy said brokenly. "I took him, and watched him assume their shape, and watched for half a day until one of them came along and took him away, poor naked child. He looked back at me but he never made a sound."

"He needs to hear the History," the Griffin said. "He needs to sit with the Midwife and hear the Darkwood tales."

"Then bring him back to me!" the Midwife Tree cried.

"Drag him?" the Fox Fairy asked. "You think that would make him understand that this is his kingdom, and not his prison? He is still afraid of us."

"There must be a way," the Unicorn said. "A gentle way."

From Charlotte Thacker's notebook

I found Miss Warder sitting wearily at the kitchen table, with one hand over her eyes. She straightened up when I walked in and attempted to smile, but there was dread in her eyes.

"I can't stand not knowing what is going on," I said quietly as I sat down. "I don't know how long it will be before we can see our parents again, but things can't go on like this. For some reason, you're playing tricks on Will and me. If you don't want us here, then just say so, and I'll call our uncle and ask him to find us another place. But it's wrong to scare us. You—you and Jonah, too . . ." I ran out of words. There was no way I could explain the strangeness in Will that had only appeared after we arrived at Gull Walk. Or the strangeness in myself. But I knew one thing for certain— Jonah was a bad influence on my brother. And the things that Miss Warder had said sounded crazy. This was a bad place.

Miss Warder touched her lips with her fingers, as if she wanted to hold words back. But then she said, "It wasn't supposed to happen like this. When Will showed up, I thought I had lost my mind."

"What do you mean?" I said sharply. I was nearly in tears, and clenching my fists to control my anger. "What about Will?"

Miss Warder sighed. "You're too young. Not even your parents know."

"Know *what?*" I shouted. I did not want to listen to anymore of Miss Warder's craziness. This was the time for truth and nothing else.

"Shh," Miss Warder hissed. She looked up at the ceiling. "The Fletchers have just gone to their room. You don't want them coming back down here."

"The Fletchers," I said. "What are they to Will? Do they know who he is? Who he *was* before my parents adopted him?"

"They suspect," she said.

"Suspect what?" I asked. I was growing tired of the

game Miss Warder seemed to be playing.

"Are you still up?" Meg asked from the doorway.

They were back from the movies! I had lost my chance now. I felt as if I had lost all of my strength, too, and I blinked back tears.

Miss Warder, clearly nervous, asked Meg how she had enjoyed the movies. Helen, coming in behind Meg, laughed and said, "We loved both films! We wish we could see them again tomorrow night."

Mr. Warder walked in last, carrying Scotty, who was sound asleep. "Three of us agreed that we had a fine time," he said. "But Scotty was bored and fell asleep before the end of the first feature."

"Oh, he always falls asleep at the movies," Helen said. She took Scotty from Mr. Warder and said she would put him to bed. "Don't start telling about it until I come back down," she told Meg. "And I get to tell about the plans for the Fourth of July parade. Two days away, and there will be fireworks! There were posters up everywhere."

Miss Warder eagerly offered to make hot chocolate for everyone, and I knew I would learn nothing more from her if she succeeded in keeping people around.

I sat down at the table to wait in frustration for my hot chocolate—and a description of the movies. When Jonah came in the back door, I barely glanced at him. He knew—oh yes! Jonah knew everything. But he and the Warders intended to keep their secrets. I hated him.

We have to leave, I decided.

"Is Will in bed?" Meg asked.

She startled me, and I nearly blurted out the truth— I did not know where my brother was.

"He was tired," I said, wondering what I would do when Meg went upstairs and found that Will was gone.

Helen came back and I endured the discussion about the movies and the town's plans for a Fourth of July parade. The hot chocolate seemed tasteless and I could not finish mine. Finally, interrupting Meg, I said I was going to bed and hurried toward the kitchen door. Everyone seemed astonished at my rudeness, and Jonah, staring, almost got to his feet. I did not look back.

Instead of going to my attic room, I slipped out of the front door into the moonlit night. I had to find Will. He would have gone to the woods, of course, this time using the beach as a path. The gravel that covered the front parking area crunched under my feet, and I stopped, afraid that the people inside would hear me. But no one came out. I waited a long moment before passing the parked cars, turning the corner of the guesthouse, and running along the strip of soft grass toward the backyard. I knew I would be visible to any- one who looked out a window, but I had no choice. I had to find Will.

When I reached the path to the gate, I slowed and did my best to move soundlessly over the ground. The gate did not creak, but the latch clicked noisily when I closed it behind me, and I froze in place. Someone must have heard that!

No one came out to look and I could see no one at any of the windows.

I began running again, this time toward the beach. I could hear my feet thumping on the dirt road, and the sound of my breathing, and even the whisper of my starched cotton skirt. Oh, let me meet Will coming back, I prayed. But I was alone on the road.

In the moonlight, I could see the quiet, persistent advance of the tide. The water looked cold and sinister, sliding higher on the sand than I had ever seen it before. I hesitated. The strip of sand and gravel between the steep bank and the water was narrow and cluttered with driftwood. Farther along the beach, a thick line of young trees grew at the top of the bank, blocking my way. I knew what lay on the other side— the area that had been logged off years ago, where stumps and alder brush would make walking hard even in daylight. I had no choice but to run along the beach and hope that the tide did not rise much more. The deep woods that attracted Will were invisible, as if moonlight could not fall there.

I moved as quickly as I could, climbing over driftwood, stumbling sometimes, and falling once so hard that I knew I had skinned both knees on wet gravel. The tide was still rising. Sometimes my shoes splashed in water.

Surely I must be close to the woods, I thought, but clouds had drifted over the moon. Walking was harder because I could see very little. This was a mistake! I should have run along the road and climbed the fence.

The water was restless now, rushing the beach in small foam-tipped waves, one after another. I would have to climb the steep bank and make my way through the brush. Stupid, stupid! I thought as I struggled upward, hanging on to rocks while my feet slid out from under me.

Suddenly I knew that someone was standing above me. I raised my head and saw two white horses, mare and colt, only a few feet away. Were they wild? I flattened myself against the cliff, hoping they were not dangerous.

"Hurry up," the colt said. "You could climb faster if you tried."

It was not a horse. It was a young unicorn! And it was speaking to me! I pressed my face against the sandy bank and held my breath. This isn't happening, I thought.

"I can't help you," the unicorn colt said. "You shouldn't be here if you can't take care of yourself. The Wyvern will get you." The creature laughed and scuffed dirt and sand down the bank over my head and shoulders.

"Hush," the mare told the colt. "Behave yourself." She bent down, then, and spoke to me in a reasonable, motherly tone that frightened me more than anything else. "Climb to the top," she said, "and don't let my daughter bother you. She likes to tease."

I had frozen in place.

"Suit yourself, then," the mare said. "You chose to come here, so you should be willing to take the responsibility for yourself."

The unicorns moved away, barely stirring the brush as they passed, and at last I looked up.

The cat sat there. "They heard you coming a long time ago," he said. "What a racket! Can you get up the rest of the way or should I call for help? You probably wouldn't like it, though. The only one big enough to pull you to the top is Wyvern, and he is very disagreeable. He hates Mudwalkers."

I shut my eyes and turned my head. I was slipping down and my hands were raw from clinging to the rocks and sand. In a moment, I thought, I would wake up and find myself in bed—perhaps even at home where I belonged—and all this would be a dream I could tell to Meg over breakfast.

"Charlotte, what are you doing?"

Will stood below me, his pale face turned up toward me.

"Will!" I cried. I looked up again, expecting to see the cat, but nothing was there. I let myself slide the rest of the way down the bank and grabbed my brother's shoulders. "I've been looking for you."

He shook my hands off impatiently. "Let's go back.

There's nothing to see down here anyway." He moved away from me and without looking behind to see if I followed, he said, "The tide's in. We're going to get wet."

I ran after him, but he kept ahead of me, never stumbling or losing his balance. The water was ankle deep most of the way, sloshing against driftwood and boulders where seaweed was tangled now. Will was nearly out of sight, but I was afraid to call out to him.

Afraid of everything now. My brother and the creatures on the cliff and the people in Gull Walk.

Afraid that I was not dreaming after all.

Something on the bank was keeping pace with me, trotting lightly, and I dared not look directly at it. It might only be a small dog, I told myself, nothing more. But what if it wasn't? The bank was not so steep here, as I grew closer to Gull Walk. Will was nearly out of sight. If he would only wait for me!

Jonah!

He had jumped off the bank and grabbed my arm. I tried to jerk away, but he was too strong.

"Let go of me!" I screamed.

"Shut up and listen!" he said, and he shook my arm. "Listen to me!"

But I tried to twist loose. He was hurting me! He would not let me go!

Will ran out of the dark and tried to push Jonah back. "Stop it!" he shouted.

Jonah let go of my arm. "I wasn't trying to hurt her.

But she can't go into the house right now. She has to wait a few minutes."

"Why?" Will demanded.

I did not wait for the answer, but I grabbed Will's hand and cried, "Run! Don't listen to him!" It seemed to me then that listening to Jonah was like listening to the cat. One could become entangled in a maze of strangeness and never find a way out.

Will ran with me, and we struggled up the bank to the road that led to the gate. If Jonah was following, I did not want to know, so I did not look back. Will opened the gate and slammed it shut behind us.

"We can't go in the kitchen," I babbled. "Everybody is in there."

"I know," Will said, panting. "I see the lights."

We hurried around to the front door and let ourselves in quietly. I heard laughter from the kitchen, and Meg saying, "Now wait a minute! That's not how it was!"

"The stairs," I whispered.

We were halfway to the first landing before I noticed that the light had burned out. The landing and the stairs above it were dark. But before I could stop Will, he had bounded ahead.

Mr. Blade stepped out of the dark.

Chapter 9

"We have missed our opportunity," the Phoenix said.

The Old Midwife Tree did not stir for a long moment, and then she groaned and said, "Why did we trust the Fox to handle this delicate matter?"

"We had no choice," the Phoenix said. "He is the only one among us who can move freely outside Darkwood. I try—"

"I know, I know," the Midwife said impatiently. Then, softening toward him, she drooped a protective branch over him. "I understand what it costs any of you to shift to one of the creatures the Chimera made. But waiting is so difficult—and I am impatient. I think we must take strong steps now."

The Phoenix shook his head. "Not kidnapping. If we frighten the Prince, he will abandon us. This is a bad time to try to coax him here, because the next days are so dangerous. And we don't know how much influence that Between has on him."

The Midwife shook half a dozen Spirit Lights out of

her branches and their agitated chirps woke the unicorn colt, who sprang up, alarmed, as if from a nightmare. Her mother nudged her fondly and the colt lay back down again and slept immediately.

"Young ones cannot be expected to be brave," she told the Midwife. "If we frighten the Prince even more than we have, we will lose."

"We have to try something!" the Midwife cried.

"We must wait for a few days," the Phoenix said. "I am sure that Fox will agree when he returns."

"If he returns," the Midwife said. "He likes staying with the Mudwalkers. You know that he does."

"He despises them," the Griffin said as he rose to his feet. "But he knows how to deal with them. When he gets back, he will agree that now we can do nothing. Too many Mudwalkers are arriving, as they always do during this season. And we must do what we always do—hide."

"I have a bad feeling," the Old Midwife moaned. "I can feel something terrible coming."

"You've been listening to the Sky Wing Spirits again," the Phoenix said. "There is nothing we can do about the distant Darkwoods. They will survive or they will not."

"If you say 'We must hope for the best,' I will squash you flat!" the Old Midwife shouted.

The surface of the pond rippled, and the creatures heard the Dragon growl. They fell silent then, miserable and frightened, and waited for the Fox Fairy to come with news.

From Charlotte Thacker's notebook

In the moment that I saw Mr. Blade, several things happened at once. Will turned toward me, terrified. Mr. Blade snarled something I could not understand and reached out both of his hands. And Jonah jumped between him and Will.

"Get back!" Jonah said.

Then I saw with horror that it was not Jonah at all, but a great tusked creature bending over Mr. Blade, claws bared and eyes fired with hatred. "Get back," it snarled.

Mr. Blade turned and ran down the dark hall. I threw my arms around my brother, terrified for both of us.

The tusked animal shimmered, and I saw Jonah again, and then a small brown grinning fox, and then the cat. I squeezed my eyes shut and held my breath. Will whimpered against my shoulder, and I could feel his thin bones and sharp shoulder blades. So small! My little brother was too young and too small for all of this.

"Yes, too young," the cat said. "But we have no choice. Listen, girl. Take him upstairs. Both of you must hide your wet clothes and get into bed. Nothing has happened, nothing that you can describe that anyone will believe. And do not leave Gull Walk, no matter what happens. Do not return to the city. Everything depends on it."

And then he ran downstairs.

I was nearly blind with fear, but I climbed the stairs with Will. Distant laughter told me that my sister and the others were still in the kitchen, but they would not stay there much longer. It was late.

"Don't turn on the light," I told Will when we reached our room. "Get out of your wet clothes, and I'll roll them up with mine and put them on the bottom of our laundry bag so Meg won't see them."

"Did you see what Jonah did? What Jonah *was*?" asked Will, his voice shaking. "He was some kind of animal."

I remembered exactly what I *thought* I had seen, but I was not prepared to admit it. I needed to think everything over carefully. Somehow Will and I had imagined something terrible. Or this was all a nightmare and I would wake up soon. "Don't talk," I told my brother. "Get into your pajamas, and don't make a sound."

Our door had a lock—and I locked it—but I was afraid that Mr. Blade might break into our room. What could we do?

If he came in, our only possible escape was the window, and we might fall if we tried to climb down to the porch roof in the dark. There was little or nothing I could do to keep Mr. Blade away from my brother.

I heard Will get into bed. I changed hastily and rolled up my wet clothes, adding Will's to the bundle, and then shoving everything into the laundry bag, rearranging dry clothes over the top. It was my turn to wash our clothes, but not until the day after the July Fourth celebration. By then the wet things might be dry. Our shoes were another problem, however. I pushed both pairs under my bed and whispered to Will that he should wear his good shoes until his others had dried.

"Meg won't like that," he said.

"Tell her you want to dress up for the holiday," I said. I pulled the bedspread down on one side so that it would hide the shoes, and then I got into bed. "Go to sleep," I told him, and then I wondered if either of us would ever sleep again.

Sleeping could be dangerous, since I was not sure I could tell the difference between waking and dreaming any longer. Determined, I lay awake and shivering under the covers until I heard the light footsteps of Meg and Helen on the stairs. Quickly, I leaped up and unlocked the door, then slipped back into bed.

Meg opened the door and whispered my name. I did not answer. Meg accepted that I was sleeping, and I listened to her clothes rustle as she took them off.

Meg fell asleep quickly, and I lay awake listening to her breathe. I can't tell her, I thought, because she will never believe a single word. I don't believe it myself.

But we had to stay away from Mr. Blade.

Morning took forever to arrive. I waited until Meg got up, and then I jumped out of bed, too, and shook Will awake. I considered whispering in his ear, telling him that he must pretend that everything was normal—but perhaps it was, in his view. If someone had asked me to swear that everything I had seen and heard the day before was true, I would not have done it. I knew—and yet I could not bear to know—and so there was nothing to do but pretend that this was only another day, like all the days since we had arrived at Gull Walk.

Helen and I helped Miss Warder with breakfast, and I tried to concentrate on what Helen said about the movies the night before. Several times, Miss Warder looked at me piercingly, as if wondering what I was thinking, but I turned away from her quickly, hiding my eyes as if Miss Warder could learn something from them.

Mr. Warder came in and said quietly, "Mr. Blade has left, and he had his suitcase with him. The Fletchers drove him away. I saw them through the window." I glanced up in surprise—and relief.

"And of course he didn't pay for his room," Miss Warder said bitterly.

Mr. Warder laughed a little. "It's happened to us before."

"Good riddance, anyway," Miss Warder said. Then she looked straight at me, and I met her gaze as long as I could.

"So Mr. Blade didn't have a car?" Helen asked. "Now that I think of it, I don't remember seeing another car outside after he came."

Mr. Warder, pouring coffee for himself in a mug, said easily, "He said he came by boat, and he left it at the Samsons' dock, so that's probably where the Fletchers took him."

"Samsons? That dumpy old fishing camp halfway to town?" Helen asked.

"It's a good place to tie up, if you're coming for the Fourth of July parade," Mr. Warder said. He was looking out the window now, and I thought that he was pretending that he was not interested in the conversation. He turned then, as if sensing my thought, and said, "We've got to make plans for our youngsters for the holiday. We'll go in for the parade tomorrow, of course, and stay for the fireworks. But how about a picnic on the beach this afternoon?"

"Wonderful!" Helen said.

I echoed that. Will would enjoy it, and I could keep watch over him easily, since he would not have an excuse to run off.

At the table in the breakfast room, the rest of them discussed the picnic eagerly. "We can go swimming!" Scotty said.

"The water is really cold, remember," Helen said.

"I don't care how cold it is," Meg said. "It's time for our real vacation to start."

Jonah did not come for breakfast, and I did not see him until later in the morning, after two families arrived, looking for rooms for the holiday. There were six children among them, two of them teenagers, and I noted bitterly that both Meg and Helen seemed to have some sort of mysterious sensory abilities that allowed them to know instantly when boys their age were in the vicinity. Before the parents had signed the registration book, Meg and Helen had introduced themselves to all of the children, with special eyelash flutterings for the two grinning boys, and they offered to show them around.

Will and I attracted the attention of three small children, who stared frankly at us until one finally asked if we owned Gull Walk.

"It belongs to friends of ours," I said. "We're staying here for a while."

This information seemed to render the children speechless, although they did not stop staring until their mothers led them off by their hands.

"Scotty ought to be happy," Will said. "He'll finally have friends his own age."

"He's lonely, isn't he?"

"Who isn't?" Will said.

He took a suitcase upstairs for the woman who was carrying a baby, and I, anxious not to be parted from him, hurried after them, followed by a small silent girl with a lollipop in her mouth.

"What's your name?" I asked her.

The little girl did not reply, but only stared at me.

❖ ❖ ❖

Will was harder to keep track of than I had expected. Miss Warder needed my help in the kitchen, and I had warned Will to stay in sight of the kitchen window. But when I looked out once, I saw him talking to Jonah, who appeared to be explaining something. He talked rapidly, his hands outspread, his head turning from side to side, probably to see if anyone was watching

I dropped the spoon I had been using to mix the salad and ran out the back door. "Will!"

He looked up at me innocently and said, "I wasn't doing anything." Whatever fears he had had about Jonah the night before were gone now, probably because of something Jonah had said to him.

"I don't want you talking to Jonah," I blurted frankly.

Jonah's sudden grin infuriated me. I darted down the steps and grabbed Will's arm. "Come inside and help out a little! You're leaving everything to Helen and Meg and me."

Will blinked, surprised, but he followed me. I looked at Jonah once more before I shoved Will into the kitchen. Jonah's grin was gone, and his eyes were piercing, unblinking, like the wary eyes of a wild animal. Perhaps—if I could get him alone—I could get answers from him.

The new guests, the McAllisters and the Winterses, willingly helped with the picnic preparations. Mr.

McAllister and Mr. Warder moved the picnic table from the side of Gull Walk to the beach, while Mr. Winters pulled apart a driftwood pile in search of logs that would make suitable places to sit. The women helped Meg and Helen carry food to the beach, with Scotty trailing behind, herding the small children as if they were sheep. The boys built a fire to roast wieners, but before we ate, all the young people went in swimming. It was safe enough, the Warders decided, since the tide was in far enough so that we could wade without worrying about sinking in over our heads if we encountered a drop-off. We teenagers splashed and swam for short periods and then ran back to the sand and our towels, shivering and laughing. The smaller children waded and picked up shells. The men watched all of us closely while the women set out food and drink on the table.

Seeing the very ordinary scene, I relaxed and even caught myself smiling. What could be wrong when people were having a picnic on the shore and everything was so normal that we could have been the figures on the cover of the *Saturday Evening Post*?

But then I realized that Jonah was nowhere to be seen. And Will never smiled. And a dozen times I had caught my brother looking far down the beach where we had been running last night.

I tried to get him aside, but he always managed to avoid me. He had been doing that all day. I watched him sharing a sandwich with Scotty and then, suddenly, I looked down the beach to the place where I had struggled so hard to get my footing and climb the sandy cliff. Something was there at the top, watching us.

A unicorn.

I looked down at the plate of salad in my lap, and when I looked up, the unicorn was gone.

Had anyone else seen it? I dared not look around.

"I hope there will be fireworks tonight," one of the youngsters said.

"There will be plenty tomorrow, after the parade," Mr. Warder said. "You'll be able to see the rockets from here." He did not sound enthusiastic.

"Oh, good!" the boys said.

But I saw Miss Warder looking down at her hands, as if she was ready to cry. And Will, instead of seeming glad, was watching the distant woods with a stricken expression.

"What's wrong?" I murmured.

"Fireworks scare the animals," he said.

It was true, I thought, remembering the neighborhood dog that had run away last Fourth of July and was never seen again. "They won't be close," I said. "It's not as if anybody would be setting off firecrackers in the woods."

"It's a dumb thing to do anywhere!" Will said angrily. "People are dumb! They scare animals and set fires and hurt everybody!"

I hushed him, because several people had glanced over at him. "We'll talk about this later," I whispered.

"No," he said, getting up. "We can't." He was still in his swimsuit and barefoot, and he began picking his way over the rocky beach, heading back toward the water.

"You can't swim now," I said, hurrying after him. "You just ate."

"I want to be by myself."

"You can't!" I exclaimed.

He turned to look straight into my eyes. "I don't belong anywhere," he said quietly. "Nothing is what I thought it was."

"I feel the same way," I said. "It's not just you—it's me, too. I don't know what's real and what isn't."

Will bent down and picked up a rock, then threw it at the water. "They tell me things, the animals in the woods. I thought maybe I was crazy, but I keep seeing and hearing them."

"It will all be over as soon as we get away from here," I said. "We won't be at Gull Walk forever. Mama will get well and Dad will come home."

"That will take too long," Will said despondently.

"Then I'll write our aunt and uncle and ask if we can go back to stay with them!" I said. "The baby will be strong enough pretty soon!"

"They didn't want us. You know they didn't."

Will was right. The chance of being able to return to

the Tate house was very small. Helen and Scotty would be going home soon, but the Thackers would be left at Gull Walk. And whatever was going on there would still be going on.

"I'll find a way to get us away from here," I said. "But in the meantime, stay away from the woods. And stay away from Jonah! I don't know who he is or what he is, but we have to stay away from him."

But Will shook his head slowly. "When I'm with him—when the Spirit Lights come—I'm glad. Then I don't think about us. About the things that are wrong."

Helen was picking her way across the rocky beach, growing close enough to hear us. "Hey, you guys," she called. "Have some dessert with us."

Sighing, Will turned back toward the beach and the picnic. "Come on, Charlotte."

At that moment, firecrackers exploded in the distance, and Will's head went up. Fright showed in his eyes.

I heard Mr. Warder say, "Early birds, down at the fishing camp."

Perhaps the Fletchers had stayed at the fishing camp, watching fireworks with their friend, Mr. Blade. I could imagine their smiles, while they hoped that something awful would happen.

The McAllister and Winters children pleaded noisily to be driven down the road to the camp so they could see the fireworks, and the two families gathered their belongings and left the beach. I was not sure if I was relieved or sorry to see them go, and I sat down with a slice of cake I did not want and tried to act as if I was enjoying myself.

"I wish we could watch the fireworks, too," Scotty said, watching Mr. Warder's face hopefully.

"Tomorrow we'll go to the parade and see the big fireworks display afterward," Mr. Warder said. Scotty was not happy with the answer, but he did not say anything else.

Helen and Meg sulked as they helped clear away the picnic leftovers. "I'll be glad when Scotty and I can go home," Helen said. "This place is so boring." If either of the Warders heard her, they did not react.

"I'm going to write Aunt Milly and ask her if we can go back with you," Meg said. "I miss my friends and I don't want to spend the whole summer here."

I could not hear Helen's response, but I knew Meg had not liked what she heard, because she stiffened and began walking back to Gull Walk alone, carrying a stack of plates.

"See?" Will said quietly to me. "Nobody wants us because we might get sick and then make them sick. And nobody wants *me*, anyway."

"Hush!" I cried. "We're your family and we want you. Something will happen to straighten all this out!"

"Oh, Charlotte," Will said. I heard the pity—and the knowledge—in his voice and I was devastated.

❖ ❖ ❖

The following day, everyone but Miss Thacker, Will, and I—and the Fletchers—went to the Fourth of July parade in town, and they stayed afterward to watch fireworks. At Gull Walk, Will and I ate dinner outside in the shade on the side of the house. I expected Jonah to show up for the meal, but he did not. Afterward, Will curled up on the back porch swing and fell asleep reading a comic book. I was grateful, because the sounds of distant firecrackers had disturbed him all day.

I sat on the top porch step and watched the shadows lengthen across the yard. Skyrockets exploded and shot up far away, and I hoped that they would not frighten the creatures in the deep woods. If unicorns really were upset about things like that. I thought about my parents, wondering what they were doing and if they were thinking of us. Worrying about us.

I'll write to Dad, I thought. Maybe he can ask to be sent back to Seattle so we can stay with him. Or maybe we can go to Hawaii to live with him. It won't matter if we have to change schools for a year. Lots of kids change schools. But Will and I can't stay at Gull Walk anymore.

Chapter 10

There was no easy way into Darkwood except by the beach below the low cliff, and sometimes, in good weather, Mudwalkers would climb up and blunder into the forest. But there were no paths there, and the brush was thick and inhospitable, so the intruders did not stay long. They never saw an animal or a bird, but sometimes they thought they heard quick movement around and behind them—rustling leaves and snapping branches, and the soft pad of feet—and so they left hurriedly even while they denied to one another that they were afraid. No one reached the pond and saw the surface rippling in the windless air. No one saw the angry eyes that watched. No one heard the Fox Fairy whispering, "Wait, brothers and sisters. Wait."

From Charlotte Thacker's notebook

The holiday passed, but a few people still came and went at Gull Walk, although they never stayed more than a night or two. The Fletchers were to blame for that—they became more disagreeable every day, picking quarrels and spying on everyone. If a new guest so much as said "Hello" to Will, the Fletchers hustled over close enough to eavesdrop. Even Helen, who seldom noticed anything that didn't concern her directly, became aware of the Fletchers' interest in my brother, and she called the couple "creepy." I couldn't have agreed more, but for reasons I couldn't explain to my cousin.

Although Gull Walk was never full, the workload increased for everybody, and even Scotty was sent out every morning to sweep the front porch and the short walk to the driveway. The Warders said they were grateful for the good weather that brought them business, but I suspected that they really did not want people staying at Gull Walk, especially now. I understood the silent tension, the dread that was mixed with hope.

"I haven't seen Jonah since—I don't even remember when," Meg said at breakfast one morning.

"He's around somewhere," Helen said indifferently as she spread jam on pancakes. "He's always skulking about."

"No, he isn't!" Meg argued.

Scotty, always upset when someone argued with his sister, stopped eating and waited anxiously to see what Helen would say next. But Helen, eyes on her breakfast, sat sullenly, her face flushed.

I sighed inwardly. No one was getting along now, or even trying. I had not seen Jonah for days—and I hoped that he had run away—but I was wise enough not to say this aloud for fear of agitating Will. I could not define his true feelings about Jonah, and I was afraid to wonder too much. Jonah could be a friend or an enemy or some kind of terrible mentor. Whether I had seen Jonah truly for what he was—some sort of enchanted creature or only a vicious tease—I wanted him a world away from my brother.

Meg, not content to let the matter of Jonah drop, said, "I asked Miss Warder yesterday where Jonah was, and she said that he was fixing something in the boathouse, but he never shows up for meals, and I haven't seen him fixing anything."

"He never did fix anything around here!" Helen retorted.

I glanced sideways at Will and saw him staring at his plate. I nudged his foot but he did not stir or change expression.

"We've all been busy," I said. "We can't keep track of everybody."

Will looked over at me angrily when I said that, and I expected him to say, "*You* keep track of *me*!" But he remained silent, and after a long moment, he returned to staring at his uneaten breakfast.

Five guests—and the Fletchers—were eating in the dining room, and the Warders were rushing back and forth, serving them. Every time Miss Warder passed the door of the breakfast room, she paused for a quick moment to look significantly at me. The last time she did this, I pushed my chair back and said, "We'd better go help in the kitchen, Meg." There was no point in saying anything to Helen, who had become surlier every day about chores.

"You come, too, Will," I added. "If you aren't going to eat."

"He'll get sick if he doesn't eat!" Helen said. "Then what? My parents won't let you move back in with us if he's sick—because of our new baby brother."

"Shut up!" Meg snapped. She picked up her plate and silverware and marched out of the room.

Will got up wearily and gathered up his table setting, but he did not say anything, and I was more worried than ever. He must not get sick!

But everything had been different after the Fourth of July. Will seemed exhausted, even though I was sure he had not gone back to the woods.

Meg and I began washing and drying the utensils the Warders used to prepare breakfast, while Will put them away. The morning was hot, so the back door stood open, and a bee buzzed on the outside of the screen door. I watched it for a moment, half-expecting it to become a living spark. But it was only a bee, and after a while it left.

"I wish Helen and Scotty would go home," Meg said finally, wringing out a dishcloth as if she were wringing Helen's neck. "I'm so sick of them! And I know that their parents will never let us go back there. Even if they didn't have the baby, they still wouldn't want us—they just don't have the courage to tell the truth. But I hate this place. I want to go home!"

I said, "I know," and then fell silent, afraid to tell her what I had done. I had written to Dad, begging him to ask if he could return to Seattle or send for us. I had told him how unhappy we were, how lonely for our own family, and how hard we would try to avoid making any kind of trouble for him. If only he would take us away from Gull Walk—or save us from having to beg to stay with the Tates. I had calculated how long the letter would take to reach him, and how long it would take for him to reply. Forever. Perhaps even too long to help Will. But I had to try, at least.

After breakfast, Meg, Helen, and I were sent upstairs to make up the occupied rooms and clean all three bathrooms, while Will and Scotty went into town with Mr. Warder for supplies.

"At least we don't have to make up the Warders' rooms," Meg said as she mopped perspiration from her forehead. The bedrooms were so hot! Opening windows did no good at all, because there was no breeze.

Helen, flapping a bedspread in place, said, "Their bedrooms are no bigger than closets." The Warders' rooms were at the far end of the second floor, flanking the staff bathroom, and they did not even have numbers on the doors like the guests' rooms.

"How do you know?" Meg challenged immediately. "Did you look?"

Helen blushed, then admitted it. "I wondered how much nicer their rooms are than ours."

"And?" Meg asked.

Helen laughed. "We're better off. We've got twice as much room, even if we are in the attic."

"Why don't they use the regular rooms then?" Meg asked. "What difference would it make? The place is never full."

"They're always hoping," Helen said.

No, they're not, I thought. They would rather the place was nearly empty most of the time. Something was wrong with Gull Walk.

Mr. Warder brought mail back from town, along with newspapers and the supplies, and he passed letters and cards to us. We hurried upstairs to read in the big attic bedroom, where we could share, out of the hearing of guests.

Helen had heard from her mother and her best friend, Meg got a letter from Dad—sent long before he could have received my letter—and I received a postcard from a girl I barely knew in school. I shoved it in my skirt pocket without reading it.

"What does Dad say?" I asked.

Meg held up her hand, signaling me to wait while she read. She nodded her head solemnly over the letter and finally said, "Dad says that Mama's doctor wrote to him and said that she won't be getting out any time soon—"

"We knew that!" I cried, exasperated.

Meg leveled an angry look at me. "Do you want me to tell you what he wrote or not?"

"Sorry," I muttered. My temper was getting worse every day.

Meg went back to the letter. "He says that he might be transferred to Manila—"

"What?" I asked, nearly in tears. "That's in the Philippines! Why would he go there?"

"Because he has to go where the Navy sends him," Meg said with a great show of patience. "You know that. But he told us before he left that he'd only be gone for a year or so, while he trained new men."

"I wish we could go with him," I said.

"Cynthia's father is in the army; he gets sent practically everywhere, and she hates it when her family goes with him," Meg said. She always had to have the last word, even when she really did not mean it. She missed Dad as much as I did.

"Maybe that Cynthia *should* hate it," Helen said. "There's going to be a war, my dad says, and maybe she could end up in some place where she'd be killed." The idea seemed to please Helen, who always managed to enjoy someone else's bad luck.

"A war!" Will said. His face had turned pale.

"Nobody knows that for sure," I said quickly. "People have been talking about it for a long time and so far nothing has happened to us."

"But still—" Helen began.

"If you don't be quiet, I'll sock you!" I shouted, losing my temper completely.

There was a long silence in the room, and then Helen tore open another envelope. "You'll be sorry you talked to me like that, Charlotte," she said. "Someday."

Will seemed stunned. "What happens to forests when there is a war?" he asked.

"Oh, they get bombed, just like everything else," Meg said. "Remember the newsreels we've seen of England?"

"But they showed bombed cities!" Will protested. "We didn't see bombed woods!"

"It's worse to bomb cities," Meg said vaguely, as she continued reading the letter. "Dad will be in the Philippines in September, and he gave an address where we can send letters." She put the letter down and looked out the window for a moment. "Somebody must think something bad really is going to happen."

"Nothing bad is going to happen," I said. "Come on, Will. Let's go down to the sitting room and find a world map. We'll see exactly where Manila is and how far away Dad will be. It won't seem so bad to us then."

"I'm coming, too," Scotty said. "I want to see Manila."

In the sitting room, we found a large world atlas, and I put my finger on the Philippine Islands and said, "This is where Dad will be."

Scotty put his finger on Seattle and said, "This is where we come from."

"It's a long way away," Meg said slowly. I could see that she was impressed now with what was happening to us. "It's too far away, much farther than Hawaii. It's clear over to the other side of the world."

I suddenly saw the possibilities of gaining Meg as an ally without telling her how important it was that Dad either come home or send for us. "Write to him," I told my sister. "He'll listen to you. Tell him to ask to come home or let us go with him."

"I don't want to go that far away!" Meg cried. "I want to go back to Seattle!"

"Then write and tell him that!" I said.

Meg looked through the letter again and then said, "He says he tried to get transferred back, but the job in Manila is so important—"

"*We're* important!" I argued.

"My father wouldn't let himself be sent so far away," Helen said smugly. "He wouldn't want to be separated from us like that."

Meg sat up straighter. "Someday, Helen," she said, "I'm going to do something to you that makes you cry."

I burst out laughing, but Helen grabbed Scotty by the arm and dragged him out of the room.

"Well," Meg said. "I'll bet Helen is going to put that in her next letter home. But I'm not sorry I said it."

"What difference does it make?" I asked, miserable and ready to cry. "You know they wouldn't have let us go back to them anyway. Write to Dad, Meg, and tell him that he has to come home."

In the middle of the afternoon, Will and Scotty settled down with comic books on the porch. Meg and Helen, still not speaking, sat in different parts of the yard, ostentatiously ignoring each other, reading their books, and sunning their bare legs. Meg had already written her letter to Dad, and it waited on the table by the front door, to be taken to the post office the following day. I thought of adding one more letter, but then I decided that Dad might feel bad if he heard anything more from me so soon. If he could do something, I was sure he would. He *had* been sorry to leave us. Now he would know that we wanted to be with him at any cost, and he would do what he could.

And if he could do nothing?

I thought for a while about the consequences of that, and then I told Miss Warder, resting in the side yard, that I was going for a walk. "Maybe to the dairy farm," I added.

"That would be nice," Miss Warder said, fanning herself with a magazine.

I left, grateful that there were enough trees between Gull Walk and the road to shield me from curious eyes. I turned toward the woods and walked rapidly. The sun was hot and the road dusty, and I was out of breath before I reached the fence enclosing the woods. I had half expected to see Jonah somewhere along the way, but he was not around, at least not in sight. Good, I thought. I did not want to deal with him now. I was already afraid of what I was planning to do, and I did not need his contempt and ridicule.

I passed the corner of the fence. The road was shaded there by the tall trees that stood between me and the afternoon sun. The scent of fir trees and ferns was sharp in the still air. I jumped across the ditch and waded through the tall grass.

And I saw a gate in the fence.

Once before I had thought that I had seen one, but I had been mistaken. Since then, I had looked at the fence every time I rode into town with Mr. Warder, and there had never been a gate.

The woods were quiet. I could hear nothing moving in them. No birds sang. Not a leaf moved.

The woods were waiting for me.

I wanted to turn and run back to Gull Walk, but there was no way I could put my fears to rest except going into the woods and deciding once and for all that there were no mystical beasts living there. No unicorns. No cat that could look like a fox. No tusked animal.

No Spirit Lights.

I pushed open the gate and walked inside. A narrow path I had never seen before led deep into the trees. I hesitated for a moment, wondering if I was making a terrible mistake, but then I took a step. I had to do this.

"Do you have an appointment?" someone asked, in a voice that seemed faintly familiar.

I clapped both hands to my mouth and stood very still, holding my breath.

"I said, do you have an appointment?" a nearby spindly birch tree asked. "You can't just barge in here as if you belonged. Either someone has given you an appointment or you'll have to leave."

I could not leave because I was too terrified. I could not even speak.

Sharp, high-pitched laughter rang out, and the tree dissolved, and a brown fox with bright eyes stood there. "What took you so long, Charlotte?" he asked. "I never thought you were the kind of girl who would stay away, just because someone told you to."

I recognized the voice! It was the cat!

I took one step backward, and the creature laughed again. "Come, come," he said. "You're here for a reason. Are you going to run home like a crybaby without finding the answers to your questions?"

My mouth was dry, but I whispered, "Who are you?"

"Ah," the fox said, and he sat down as if preparing to deliver a long and complicated speech.

"Don't get him started!" another voice shouted. Twigs and leaves rattled down on me, and I cringed. An old, hollow tree was doing it! "Don't ask him anything, because he doesn't know anything. Now that you're here, come inside and see for yourself."

My hands shook and I clasped them together. "Who are you?" I asked again. I longed to look behind me, to see if there was anyone on the road who might help me if I screamed.

"No one is there to help you," the Unicorn said. "You are alone here with us, but we won't hurt you." The white animal stood half hidden behind a tree, with her colt by her side. "Come along. Walk on the path the Fox Fairy made for you when we heard you coming. We'll show you everything."

"Everything!" cried dozens of Spirit Lights. They clustered around me, chattering, but I did not understand anything else they said.

"Idiots!" the old hollow tree cried, and she swatted at them with a branch. They fled, complaining, deep into the forest. "Not everyone here is intelligent, you know," she told me in a confidential tone. "I am the Old Midwife, and everything I say is true. We're divided up just like the Mudwalkers—half idiots and fools, and half intelligent beings. I hope you weren't silly enough to expect something better! After all, the Chimera who caused all the trouble—"

"Don't tell her about all that now," the Fox Fairy

said. "Wait until we get to the pond."

"Oh, have it your own way!" the old tree said, and she wrenched her roots out of the forest floor and plodded down the path, ahead of me.

"Come on," the Fox Fairy said, and he nudged my leg with his cold nose. "Hurry up."

I followed the lurching tree down the path, deep into the forest, until I reached a clearing. In the middle, there was a dark, still pond. The trees ringing the pond were filled with Spirit Lights and other colorful creatures that seemed almost birdlike. As they fluttered, they changed colors, and sometimes I almost thought I recognized some of them. The unicorn colt charged a bush and a terrible beast sat up and stretched and yawned, as if waking from a nap.

"She's here?" it rumbled. "About time."

"This is Phoenix," the Fox Fairy said. "And over there is Wyvern. Don't let him worry you. And behind you is Gryphon and Pooka. There are many others here who do not choose to be seen by you. All of our mothers were brought to birth of us by the Old Midwife, so we owe her our respect—even though sometimes this is hard." Leaves showered on him and he ignored them. "We would have sent for Kelpie, but she is very far away."

"I'm dreaming a fairy tale," I muttered.

"Of course," the Fox Fairy said. "What else could *you* be doing? All Mudwalkers do is dream that they are real. Just a few of them can see what *you* see, but even they never seem to understand that they themselves are nothing more than clumsy toys."

"Sit down," the Gryphon told me, gesturing to a log near the pond.

I sat, and a dozen Spirit Lights immediately clustered around me and came to rest in my lap. They felt warm between my hands, sparks that could not burn.

The water in the pond rippled. "Get to the point," a deep voice rumbled from underneath it. "Let the Old Midwife talk. She knows the history."

"Once upon a time," the Old Midwife Tree began, only to be met with hoots of laughter.

"If you're going to tell it that way, I'm leaving," Gryphon said, and he began to rise to his feet.

The Old Midwife Tree thrashed her branches, and I brushed leaves out of my hair, afraid to complain.

"Why don't you ask her if she has questions?" the Unicorn said in her reasonable, motherly tone. "Children always have so many questions. Sometimes it's easier to explain things if you just answer them."

The creatures waited, watching me. I clenched my hands together tighter. "What is this place?" I asked finally.

"Darkwood!" several said at once.

"This is the *real* world," the old tree said. "In the beginning, the forests were all there was, the forests and those of us who were created at the same time. And we lived forever and forever, until one day a Chimera—"

"Wretched, ungrateful beasts!" the Phoenix cried.

"Until a Chimera decided to play a game. He made creatures out of sand and mud and water to resemble the Fair Ones and set them to play on a beach somewhere—"

"Tell her who the Fair Ones are!" the Fox Fairy demanded. "Otherwise, your ramblings don't make any sense at all."

"The Fair Ones are . . ." The Old Midwife seemed to be at a loss for words. "The Fair Ones look like Mudwalkers, only they are beautiful, not ugly like you—"

"Well, that's a help," the Fox Fairy said disgustedly. "Why don't you call her Four Eyes and be done with it."

I looked at him sharply. I had forgotten for a moment that he was the cat. And perhaps he was even Jonah.

"All right," the Old Midwife said. "The Fair Ones are beautiful, and the Chimera could not make anything exactly like them, especially since his building material was the mud he found on beaches everywhere. But he tried. And then he made Mudwalker animals, crude imitations of the true creatures of the forests. But, you see, not one of the Mudwalkers was immortal. They all died after a while, and what the Chimera did was quite cruel, because they all had feelings of one sort or another. Crude feelings. Still, he should not have done it.

"And then, one day, the Mudwalkers who looked

almost like the Fair Ones realized what they really were. Only ugly copies of perfection. And they set about trying to kill the Fair Ones and the true creatures of the forests. But they could not. We are immortal, as long as we have contact with the nurturing forests. And so they began burning and cutting down the forests, and we became weaker and weaker, and many of us disappeared—we don't know where—until only a few of us are left. And the Darkwoods have lost contact, because the Sky Wings are too weak to fly the great barren distances between forests to carry messages. In order to protect ourselves, we learned to change our shapes, so that we resembled Mudwalker animals. Oh, they would kill them, certainly. Mudwalkers kill so casually. If one of us was caught in Mudwalker form, we would die.

"And then one day the Mudwalkers came here. They came in late winter, when we were weakest, and cut trees, so many trees . . ." She sighed, and I had to wait a while before the old tree could go on. "There was nothing anyone could do. They had stronger weapons. A few of them had the power to see us as we really are, and they wanted us dead. The others—they only wanted to destroy Darkwood. All the Darkwoods everywhere, until the earth is fit only as a place for Mudwalkers. And then, of course, the world will all end. That is the rule that cannot be broken. The world will end."

I waited. The old tree was silent.

"What does my brother have to do with this?" I asked finally.

"He is the last of the Fair Ones that lived here," the old tree said sadly. "His parents died in the last invasion. Many of us died because so many of the trees were cut down. Your brother was sent out to the road to take Mudwalker form and wait for one of you to take him in. It has been done before."

"I guarded him until the car came!" the Fox Fairy cried defensively, as if he had been accused of something. "He was not left out there alone. A car came and took him away, and then we began the long wait."

"Let me tell it," the old tree said. "Yes, we waited, because we knew that he would be drawn back, once he was grown. They always are. They can't resist going back to the forests, even if they never learn why. We expected our Prince to return to us, but not so soon."

Prince? I thought. My brother?

"He returned too soon," the Wyvern said, lashing his tail angrily. "He is too young to be of help."

"No, he is not!" the Phoenix said.

"He is!"

"Quiet!" the Dragon roared from deep below the pond. The water stirred violently and a dozen small orange creatures leaped out of it, squeaking in protest.

The old tree sighed. "The Dragon will hatch when the Prince joins us. Every Fair One has a dragon."

I stared.

"That is how it has always been," the Fox Fairy said. "Not even we know why, but it is always true. Every Fair One has a dragon."

I slumped wearily on the log. "You—all of you—are like creatures in a child's picture book. How can I believe you?"

"Then don't believe," the Old Midwife Tree said angrily. "Sooner or later our Prince will return to us, strong enough to help us, and it won't matter what you believe or don't believe."

I looked down at my hands, almost wondering if they were made of mud. I held them out to the tree and said, "Look. I'm flesh and blood, not sand and water."

"So *you* think," the tree said.

"We told you that you are dreaming," the Fox Fairy said. "Everything that happens to you is only a dream, because you are not real."

"If I'm not real—if *people* are not real—then why can we hurt you?" I asked.

"You kill the trees," everyone said. "Yes, *you* kill the trees."

"If we aren't real, how *can* we?" I asked.

"The Chimera made you filled with hatred for beautiful things," the Old Midwife Tree said. "Hatred is the most powerful weapon. It was his little joke, he said. You were to be his toys. But you got away from him, and when we saw what he had done, a dragon put an end to him."

"How could he?" I asked. "If you can only be destroyed when trees are cut down, how could anything destroy a Chimera?"

"Like this!" the Fox Fairy said, and suddenly I saw a scene, almost like something projected on a movie screen, and there before me a hideous beast was being dragged into deep water by a Phoenix, and the Phoenix held him firmly even though he struggled, and after a while orcas came and pulled him away, far away to the sea, where days and nights cycled, light and dark, and finally the Chimera disappeared, fading into nothingness. The orcas leaped joyously, and then they changed to mermaids and they dived deep, and the sea was still . . . still . . . still.

"You see? A Chimera must have contact with a forest, too," the Fox Fairy said. "If one is deprived, he dies."

"But there was another time," the Old Midwife said, "when a Chimera was enchanted by a powerful Dragon who turned him into a black bear, and a Mudwalker came and shot him. Somewhere, he is— "

"A rug," the Wyvern said with a hoot of laughter. He rolled over on his back and kicked his two legs in the air. The Spirit Lights tittered with laughter.

I gasped. "That's terrible."

"That is justice," the Fox Fairy said. "He was forced to accept a form that another Chimera had invented, and he paid the price that his kind designed. So it is— and so it is."

"If we can survive long enough, the Mudwalkers will all destroy themselves, and we will be free," the Phoenix said. "Now do you see?"

I shook my head. "What does this have to do with Will?"

All the creatures sighed. "If he is to be an immortal, he must join us," the Fox Fairy said. "And to join us, he must give up the Mudwalker world. Time is short. Some of us are afraid . . ."

"*All of us* are afraid," the Unicorn said. "Can you let him go? The Fair Ones are our natural leaders. We need him."

I sat very still for a moment, and then I got up and walked away. I could think of nothing to say. What they wanted was terrible. They wanted my brother.

The path closed behind me as I walked. I looked back once and saw the underbrush rustling into place, hiding my footsteps. The forest looked as if I had never been there. As if I did not really exist. After I stepped through the gate, it swung shut and melded into the fence—and was gone.

A gull cried overhead. I looked up and wondered what it was that I was seeing, a real gull or a mystical creature from Darkwood.

"Help us," the gull cried. "Charlotte, please help us."

I ran.

Chapter 11

The Unicorn and her colt trotted into the clearing, where the Wyvern was sleeping. She nudged him awake and said, "Someone evil is coming. We saw him from the cliff."

The Wyvern jumped up. "Someone is on the beach?"

The Fox Fairy burst through the underbrush. "I saw him! The one who smelled like a Chimera! And he has brought hunters with him."

A cloud of Spirit Lights flew up, chattering in terror. In the distance, the Old Midwife Tree bellowed, "Who is coming? Who is it?"

"Chimera! Chimera!" a dozen voices cried.

"Send the Sky Wings to the ocean and tell the Kelpie!" the Old Midwife called out. "Tell her we are under attack again!"

"There might not be time!" the Fox Fairy cried. "The Chimera is coming for the Prince."

A dozen Sky Wings soared overhead and turned west, toward the ocean. More followed.

"Bring the Prince here until the Kelpie comes," the Gryphon told the Fox Fairy, who turned and ran.

"Then the end has come," the Old Midwife said, suddenly subdued.

The colt huddled close to her mother, and all of them watched the sky until the Sky Wings were out of sight. The Kelpie would come—and who could tell what form she would take—but the Prince could be lost to them.

The water in the pond boiled, and out of it rose the young Dragon, his golden eyes filled with lightning, his mouth filled with thunder. He twisted his silver neck and roared, and he called forth a sudden storm. Wind lashed the trees, and beyond, the Sound surged and pounded the beach.

"The Chimera has set the time," the Dragon shouted, "but we will begin the battle!"

FROM CHARLOTTE THACKER'S NOTEBOOK

It seemed to me that I had been gone for hours, but only a short time had passed. Meg and Helen were still in the yard, reading—and ignoring one another, if that could describe sidelong glances and noisy sighing. Will and Scotty were still busy with comic books on the back porch, but Will looked tired and barely glanced at me when I opened the screen door to check on him.

The Warders had been in the kitchen, beginning dinner preparations, when I returned home, and Miss Warder smiled a little when I first entered. I had hoped to find her alone, but I would have to wait for another opportunity. I did not want to speak of Darkwood in front of Mr. Warder yet.

I asked what I could do to help, and Mr. Warder asked me to begin salad preparations. Miss Warder, scrubbing potatoes at the sink, did not look up to meet my gaze.

She knows she's guilty, I thought angrily. She knows what she's done by not warning us as soon as she knew. By not telling Uncle Ned that we could not stay here, once she knew about Will.

But what could she have said? I wondered miserably. I did not even know what I could have said. I only knew that Will must leave this place as soon as possible. How could I bring this about?

"We received a telegram while you were gone," Miss Warder said without looking up. "The Tates want Helen and Scotty put on the bus back to Seattle tomorrow morning."

I gasped. Helen and Scotty? Not the Thackers, too? I could only babble helplessly, saying, "But what about us? They can't mean to leave us here! My dad wouldn't want us to be left here!"

"You're welcome to stay here for as long as you want," Mr. Warder said cheerfully. But he did not look up from the meat he was getting ready for the broiler. "You can stay until your father returns."

"Uncle Ted and Aunt Milly didn't want us, did they?" I asked, humiliated, my mouth so dry that I could barely speak.

"Well, dear, with the new baby and all . . ." Miss Warder began. Her voice trailed away and she looked at me pitifully. "I'm so sorry, Charlotte. Under the circumstances, this is—"

"You can't let this happen!" I cried. "You have to do something to help Will. Send a telegram to my uncle and tell him that he has to take Will back, at least!"

But the Warders looked down, avoiding my eyes. "It won't do any good," Mr. Warder said. "Read it for yourself, Charlotte."

He pulled the folded yellow sheet from his pocket and handed it to me. I blinked away tears and read the damning words for myself. Uncle Ted had made himself clear. "Thacker children must not return here."

I would never forgive him! I handed back the telegram. "Did you tell anyone yet?" I asked.

"Not yet," Mr. Warder said. "We were waiting for you to return. You seem to be the strongest."

"I'm not!" I cried. "I'm not! You know about Will. Both of you. You know we can't stay here!"

"We'll do what we can," Miss Warder said. She wiped a potato dry, set it aside, and picked up another. "We will write to your father immediately and see if he can make other plans."

"It will take forever to hear from him—and he's going to Manila!" I wept. "What could he do?"

Miss Warder put her arms around me. "Give us a little time. We'll protect Will. We won't let him go to the woods."

"You can't watch him every moment! Sometimes he wants to be there! You can't tie him up to keep him here, because you know that Jonah will take him back if he wants to go. Jonah! Why do you let him stay here when you know what he is?"

"We let him stay because we *do* know," Miss Warder said. "When we were children, our parents showed us the creatures in the woods, and we promised them we would guard them all our lives. But after most of the trees were cut down, and the hunters went in . . . Jonah has been the messenger between the worlds, while we all waited for Will to return. We thought he wouldn't come back until he was grown."

"You must know what the Fletchers are!" I said.

"Hunters," Mr. Warder said. "They have been coming here for years, watching for the creatures. And Jonah has watched them. They've seldom caught even a glimpse of the creatures, and never long enough to do much harm. Friends of theirs have offered us a fortune for the woods, but we will never sell them. The greatest danger has always been that they would one day find someone like Mr. Blade. Someone determined to end it all."

"Then why didn't you close Gull Walk?" I asked angrily.

"There are other places the Fletchers could stay," Mr. Warder said. "As long as they were here, we—and Jonah—could watch them."

I shuddered. "Mr. Blade is almost like one of the Darkwood creatures, only evil."

"There are bad creatures as well as good," Miss Warder told her. "The Chimera were always the worst, from the beginning of time. It was one of them who made us."

"I know," I said bitterly. "We were just a joke that got out of hand."

"Yes," Miss Warder said. "A terrible joke on the world."

Will and Scotty came in the back door then and asked for lemonade. Will avoided looking directly at me, took a glass, and disappeared toward the sitting room.

"The sky has turned all black," Scotty said as he reached for the glass I held out. "It's windy now, too."

Meg came in, brushing her hair back in place with one hand. "A terrible wind has come up. It practically blew me off the steps. We're going to have a storm."

Lightning flashed then, followed by a roar of thunder. Helen ran through the door. "I could see lightning over the Sound," she said. "It's beautiful and scary, both at the same time. I love a big storm like this."

Scotty returned, looking puzzled. "Where's Will? I thought he was going into the sitting room."

"He must be upstairs then," I said, and I started toward the back stairs. I did not want to run—it was ridiculous to think that Will would leave Gull Walk during a storm—but I was afraid that he might have done exactly that, so I stumbled upstairs as fast as I could.

Will was sitting on the edge of his cot, lemonade glass in one hand and *Nine Thousand Dragons* in the other. He stared at me, astonished. "What do you want?"

"I thought you were going in the sitting room," I said.

Thunder roared again. "I changed my mind," Will said. He sounded surly now. "Sometimes I like to be alone."

Lightning flickered outside the window, and thunder exploded at almost the same second. Will looked down at his book, and I thought that he was becoming quite good at ignoring people when he wanted to shut them out of his life.

But then, why should he not do that? He wasn't like me. He wasn't human. Oh, it was not believable! Not bearable!

"How much do you know?" I asked him, knowing that he would understand the question completely.

Thunder shook the window. "I know everything," Will said, and then he added in a softer voice, "I'm sorry, Charlotte."

"Sorry about what?" I asked as I sat down next to him.

"About everything. About not being what you wanted. About going away."

"You *can't* go away!" I said. "What would Mama think if she lost you?"

Will's expression was pitying. He seemed older suddenly, older than I. Older than anyone. Older than the world. "Someday it won't matter," he said.

Rain lashed the window for a moment, and then it stopped. The sky lightened, and the last roll of thunder was far away.

"They've won for now," Will said. "Darkwood won. But Mr. Blade—and the Fletchers—are still out there, waiting for me."

I sat down beside him and said, "They won't get you."

"They will if I stay here," Will said, and he sounded resigned, as if whatever was to happen was beyond his power—beyond anyone's power. "I'm not strong enough—and the Darkwood creatures aren't strong enough—to fight someone like Mr. Blade if I stay outside the woods."

I was afraid to say what I thought, but Will spoke the words instead. "No matter where I go or what I do, someone will be hurt. If I go to Darkwood, Mama and Dad will be so afraid. No one will believe what happened. No one will understand. So they will think that something terrible happened to me. But if I stay with you, the Chimera will find me sooner or later. The Fletchers will help him. Either way, the end will be the same for Mama and Dad. And you and Meg. I can't make it different for any of you."

I saw that he was even thinner than before, his skin whiter, his eyes darker. His hair had grown too long and curled around his ears. He looked like what he was—not human. Did the others see?

"But you can make it different for yourself," I said.

"I guess so." He sounded tired now. "I can try to hide forever, the way others have done." He drank the last of his lemonade and lay back on his cot. "I don't want any dinner. Tell them I don't feel very well."

"Will you be here when I come back upstairs tonight?"

"Yes." He shut his eyes.

By the time I reached the kitchen again, the Warders had told the others about the telegram. Helen and Scotty were elated. Meg slumped at one end of the kitchen table, looking devastated.

"I want to go back, too," she said. "Bonnie told me that her parents said I could stay with them. I'll write to her tonight."

What about Will and me? I thought. But I said nothing, knowing what the answer would be. Enough of this! I thought. If there was a solution, I could not imagine it. I offered to set the tables in the dining room and carried the plates out of the kitchen. Behind me, I could hear Miss Warder asking the question that I had not asked: What about Will and Charlotte?

I did not want to hear Meg's answer, because I knew it would make me cry.

The Fletchers came in while I was setting their table. Mrs. Fletcher wore a tight smile, and she raised her eyebrows when I glanced over at her. I longed to say, "You lost today," but I knew better. Will was safer if the Fletchers were uncertain about how much help he had.

In the middle of the night, I awoke to find the cat sitting next to me on the bed. "Don't worry," he whispered. "Trust me. Trust *us*."

I turned my face into my pillow and pushed him away.

After breakfast the next day, Mr. Warder drove Helen and Scotty to town to catch the bus. Helen promised to faithfully write to us every week, giving us the latest news of the baby and all our friends. Meg muttered, "Don't bother," under her breath. We stood in the driveway, waving halfheartedly until the car disappeared.

"I have always hated Helen," Meg said. "Just see if I ever send her a birthday or Christmas card again."

I was too bitter to respond. We trailed back into the house to start the morning chores. "I'll help Will with his share," I told Meg. I did not want to say that I was afraid to let him out of my sight.

"I think the Warders should take him to a doctor," Meg said. "He's beginning to look sick."

"The hot weather bothers him. The storm didn't help a bit."

It was easy to persuade Meg to take care of the bedrooms while Will and I took care of the bathrooms. I let Will sit on the floor, leaning against the wall, while I did all the work. He did look sick, but I was sure that this was not a sickness that any doctor could fix.

Finally I asked, "Do you want to go back to Darkwood?"

He nodded wearily. "But it scares me, too, even if I feel better when I'm there. I feel stronger."

If what the creatures said was true, then of course Will would feel stronger when he was in the woods. Pretending to be one of us—that would be exhausting.

"Wait until Meg leaves," I said. "She'll probably go to Bonnie's. Then we'll be alone with the Warders, and you can spend more time in the woods."

"If I go in, maybe I can't come back," he said.

"Jonah does! He comes and goes whenever he feels like it. You must be at least that strong, once you learn how to do whatever he does to change shape."

But Will closed his eyes and leaned his head back. "I'm afraid that I'm not that strong," he said. "I've been away too long."

❖ ❖ ❖

Later in the afternoon, while Will and I were picking berries at the end of the garden, Jonah appeared suddenly. "The Chimera is back, at the fishing camp. He brought more hunters with him this time."

"They can't hunt in summer!" I exclaimed. "Nobody hunts in summer."

"They'll do as they please," Jonah said. "They always do. They won't count on getting caught."

"Then you'll have to do something! All of you!"

"There aren't enough of us," Jonah said. "We aren't strong enough unless the Dragon comes out of the pond to stay. And he will not leave the pond again unless Will promises to commit himself to us. That is the Law. The Dragon belongs to the Fair Prince and only him. The Prince must accept his part. If we don't have the Dragon's strength, we can't win. We are afraid the Mudwalkers will set fire to the woods. They've done it before, in many places."

"Fire? Then Will can't go there!" I cried.

"Without him, we cannot fight!" Jonah snapped. "He must come."

"He's only a boy!" I said.

Will staggered against me and nearly fell. I caught him and said, "See? He hasn't enough strength to help you."

Jonah's eyes flashed with anger. I could see the fox in him. And something else, something larger, more terrifying. "He is weak because he has to remain a Mudwalker! *You* are making him do this! This is *your* fault!"

I half dragged Will toward the garden gate. "Don't look back," I told him. "Don't talk to Jonah. We need time to think."

But I was so frightened now that my teeth chattered. I had no choice but to tell Miss Warder. There had to be a way to get Will away from here, even if it meant sending us to Seattle to stay in a hotel.

Will pulled back. "Charlotte, what will happen to Darkwood?"

"I don't care!" I said. "Come on, Will. Let's get inside the house."

He went with me, but he looked ready to cry. The creatures he called Spirit Lights followed us halfway, but then they faded and disappeared.

Meg met us at the back door. "Get in here and help me right now, Charlotte!" she said. "Dinner is almost ready, and the dining room tables haven't been set yet."

"I have to talk to Miss Warder," I said.

But Meg would not listen. "Three ladies checked in half an hour ago, and they want dinner, too. And the Fletchers are complaining . . ."

It seemed impossible to me that anything like real life could be happening anywhere in the world. The Warders were busy in the kitchen and barely looked up at us. Meg shoved a tray of plates and silverware at me. "I'll clean Will up and send him in to set our table in the breakfast room. Hurry up, Charlotte! I have to finish the salads!"

Miss Warder smiled at me, but her eyes told me that she was as worried as I was.

I carried the tray into the dining room and set the tables quickly. Three older women stood by the windows overlooking the side yard, talking softly among themselves. They smiled at me. They were not frightening.

But the Fletchers waited outside the door that led to the hall, and their eyes were sharp and cruel. "Where's the boy?" Mrs. Fletcher called out to me. "How is he feeling today? Sick again?"

"He's completely well," I lied as I finished setting the table nearest the door for them. "Perfectly well and strong. Boys get over things quickly, don't they?"

They did not answer me. Of course they did not want Will strong. He would be harder to catch.

I'd had to lie to them, but all I could think of was Will's thin, pale face, his weariness. The hopelessness of his position.

"How much longer are you planning on staying?" I asked them suddenly.

I had caught them off guard. Mr. Fletcher said nothing, but Mrs. Fletcher snapped, "What a rude girl you are! What business is it of yours?"

I turned to face them and said, "I heard that Mr. Blade is back in the area. I thought you might be joining him, since there's not much for you to do around here."

"There's plenty to do around here," Mr. Fletcher rumbled, looking at me from under his eyebrows.

"I can't imagine what," I said. "Except things that shouldn't be done."

They looked at me for a long moment and I was determined to stare them down. Finally they glanced toward their table, as if they were ready to sit down at last.

"Be careful what you eat," I said. "Very careful of what you eat tonight."

I had startled them. Good! Mrs. Fletcher's mouth opened and closed as if she wanted to answer me but could think of nothing to say. Then Mr. Fletcher grabbed her arm and yanked her away, toward the front door and out of Gull Walk.

Were they going to town? Or were they joining Mr. Blade?

Chapter 12

"You cannot remain like this," the Griffin told the Old Midwife Tree. "We need everyone now, the youngest and the oldest, and even you."

Night had fallen in Darkwood, and the creatures had gathered by the pond to plan—and to comfort one another. No one knew what might happen next.

The Old Midwife sighed and wrenched her roots from the ground. "I know you are right. I know that my end must be near—"

"No!" a dozen voices cried.

"There are too few of us," the Old Midwife said. "Too much of the forest has been cut, and we are weak and alone. Our Fair Prince is too young and too frightened to save us. It's time we faced that his coming here too soon has made him vulnerable to the Chimera—and those Betweens who are evil—and there is nothing we can do."

"I have not given up," the Fox Fairy said. "I even hope that the good Betweens will find a way to stand with us. But, Midwife, the Chimera is waiting for the right time to attack, so you must change now." He was kinder than usual, perhaps realizing that the battle to come might mean the end to all of them. "It must be now."

Darkwood seemed to tremble slightly as the Old Midwife Tree struggled to resume her true shape. The unicorn colt watched, amazed, as the tree grew taller, and thinner, and shed leaves and branches. Then she stretched even taller, and the colt was looking up at a great, shining, winged serpent with a jeweled face so glorious that she was difficult to watch. It was like looking straight into a brilliant sunrise.

A dozen creatures stepped out of the shadows to greet her, shy beings who were rarely seen by anyone. The Old Midwife bent down to speak quietly to each one. Each of them took on a strange radiance at her words.

"Are we going into battle now?" the unicorn colt asked. Her voice trembled. Her mother rubbed her face against the colt's neck and murmured, "Not you, small one. You will watch from the cliff."

"I don't want to be alone!" the colt cried. "Don't leave me here alone!"

"Poor child," several creatures said sadly. "But what can be done?"

"She must learn to be brave," her mother said. But her eyes had filled with tears.

The great serpent bent down and whispered something in the unicorn colt's ear, and the youngster stood *a little taller. Her silky coat took on a bright sheen. "I can do that," she said whispered back.*

"What did you tell her?" the Fox Fairy asked the Old Midwife.

"That I brought her into this world to serve the needs of the Prince when he returned, and she is old enough now."

But the Fox Fairy worried that they would not survive the night.

FROM CHARLOTTE THACKER'S NOTEBOOK

I hurried toward the kitchen to tell the Warders that the Fletchers had gone, but Jonah reached out from the shadows and grabbed my arm. "They've left?" he asked hoarsely.

I stared at him. He looked exhausted—and weak. The hand that held my arm trembled.

"What's wrong with you?" I asked.

"Have they left?" he asked again, urgently.

I nodded. "But I don't know where they went or when they're coming back."

Jonah let go of my arm and pushed his rough hair away from his forehead. "They will join Blade. The Chimera."

He was not making much sense. "Are you sick?" I asked. "You look terrible."

"I can't stay away from Darkwood for very long," he said. "None of us can."

"Will can! He has, for years!"

"He is a Fair One, and they have greater powers. But even he is growing weak, now that he has learned that he is not a Mudwalker. The truth is destroying him because his loyalties are divided between the two worlds."

"I want to take him away from here," I said.

"Then he will die," Jonah said. "You never should have brought him here in the first place unless you wanted him to be reunited with us."

"I didn't bring him here!" I protested, tears stinging my eyes. "We had no choice. And no one knew what he was."

Jonah sighed. "I'm going back to the woods," he said. "When the trouble starts—and it will, tonight—let the Prince decide if he wants to help us or not. *You* let him make up his own mind. Otherwise, the responsibility for the losses will all be yours. You will know—but you still will go ahead and help the Chimera and his evil toys."

He ran off down the hall and left by the front door. In my mind, I could see him in the shape of the fox, padding quickly toward the forest.

I went to the kitchen and told the Warders that the Fletchers had left and I did not know if they were coming back.

The old couple looked at each other and then at me. But before they could speak, Will came in. "I've finished setting the table in the breakfast room," he said. "What's wrong?"

"Nothing, nothing at all," Miss Warder said. "Dinner is ready, so you might as well sit down."

I carried the tray of food into the small room and Meg joined us, pale and fretful. "I go to all the trouble of setting places for the Fletchers and they seem to have disappeared. Did you say something to them, Charlotte?"

Will looked at me strangely. "I didn't say anything that matters," I said. "Meg, do you want potatoes or rice?" It was nearly impossible to pretend that nothing was wrong.

Meg served herself from the tray and sighed. "I wish I could have gone back to Seattle with Helen and Scotty."

"You'll be leaving soon enough," I said. I had difficulty concentrating on her complaints. All I could think of was the Fletchers joining up with Mr. Blade somewhere—and perhaps others like them—and the danger that Will was in, unless I could think of something.

None of us ate much. From the other room, I heard the Warders talking to the three women. Everything sounded peaceful enough, deceitfully peaceful.

When will this end? I wondered. How can it end?

❖ ❖ ❖

Meg helped the Warders clear up after dinner, and I sat with Will in the breakfast room, playing checkers. Neither of us concentrated on the game. Twilight seemed to be drawn out longer that night. The air inside Gull Walk was stuffy and smelled of the chicken we had eaten for dinner.

"I have to go outside," Will said suddenly. "I can't breathe in here. And I can't stand not knowing what's going on."

"You can't go out," I whispered. "It's dangerous."

"It's dangerous in here, too," he said. "It's dangerous everywhere. Can't you understand that, Charlotte? What's happening here is happening all over the world, in all the places I read about in the magazines . . . all the places we read about in the newspapers. All the Darkwoods are vanishing. All the creatures. All . . ." His voice faded and stopped.

"And all the Fair Ones like you," I finished for him. "You're talking about the wars, aren't you?"

He shrugged impatiently. "What difference does it make? Mudwalker wars or Mudwalker selfishness or Mudwalker jealousy."

He's using their language now, I thought. He's slipping away from me.

He stood, but I leaped up and reached across the table, trying to grab him. "Please!" I cried.

He stopped, looking down at his feet. "Charlotte . . . "

he began. But he shook his head in exasperation and hurried away toward the back door.

Both the Warders tried to stop him—I heard them cry his name—but the door banged behind him. As I reached the kitchen, they looked at me imploringly. "He shouldn't have left," Miss Warder said. "Blade and the Fletchers wouldn't do anything to him here, in front of strangers."

"I'll go after him," I said, but I was frightened half out of my wits.

"We'll all go," Miss Warder said. She and her brother followed me out to the porch.

All three of us saw the woman at the same time. She was extremely tall, with long, light brown hair, and she was walking up the road from the beach. The long black coat she wore blew out behind her in the wind, showing the thin brown dress she wore underneath. Her feet were bare.

Will ran toward her as if he recognized her. She bent and embraced him, and then looked back at us.

"It's time," she said clearly.

And then she and Will walked away together, toward the beach and the woods beyond.

"We can't let him go off with her!" I cried. "We don't know who she is. She could be one of the Chimera, or someone the Fletchers sent."

But the Warders seemed amazed, as if they were witnessing something incredible.

"She is the Kelpie," Miss Warder said finally. "They must have sent for her and she's come to help them."

"We'd better go down to the beach and see what's going on," Mr. Warder said. "We might be able to help, too."

"Not Charlotte!" Miss Warder said. "She must stay here. She's only a child."

"Will is my brother," I said. "I'm going, even if I have to go alone."

I ran ahead of them, easily outdistancing them. The tide was out, and the long wet beach stretched out toward what looked like the end of the world but was only the dark water pulling away. The sky was overcast. The night that was falling would be completely black.

I hurried along the rocky beach, hoping to catch sight of my brother and the seal woman, but they must have climbed the cliff somewhere. I passed the violated area where the trees had been cut. Ahead, Darkwood loomed black in the deepening gloom. I would climb the high bank here, I decided.

A hand reached down from above. Jonah. "We need you," he said, and he pulled me up, to stand beside him. "They are here," he said. "All of them, the Chimera and the Fletchers and some other people, evil Betweens. They are coming down the beach from the fishing camp."

"What can they do?" I said.

"Burn Darkwood," he said. "They think they are immortal, and fire has always been their favorite tool." Before my eyes, he changed into the fox.

But the moment he changed, I saw the first flames flickering at the far corner of Darkwood. Where was Will?

It was too dark for me to see a path. The fox darted ahead of me, plunging into the brush, and I had no choice but to follow him. Behind me, I heard the voices of the Warders, calling out to me to wait for them. But I seemed to have become almost as skillful as the fox in slipping between trees and through the thick brush.

"Fire!" I heard someone cry, and the Unicorn mother and her child ran past us, going in the opposite direction. "They've brought fire!"

"Will! Where are you?" I screamed. I could hear the fire crackling in the underbrush now. A long brown creature that seemed part lion and part eagle ran from behind me, passing me and lunging away from the woods where the fire was now climbing into the trees.

Will did not answer my shouts. No one answered. The fox had outdistanced me and was out of sight. I looked to my right and saw, through the trees, what seemed to be torches at the edge of Darkwood. It had to be the Fletchers and Blade, setting more fires as they went along the edge of the cliff.

Without thinking, I pushed my way through, toward them. They had to be stopped.

Then I saw Will ahead of me, a different Will, even more delicate than before, his skin turned silver. "Will!" I shouted.

He stopped to look back at me. "Go away, Charlotte," he said. "This is our battle."

"I'll help you!" I shouted. "I'll do anything!"

And then I saw the creature that accompanied him. It rose up nearly as high as the tallest tree, and it turned its flaming eyes toward me. A dragon. Will's dragon had hatched.

Wings beat the air. A serpent came to rest in the top of a tree and bent her head down to stare, almost in my face. "You," she said, and she sounded disgusted. "All right. You're better than nothing. Come along, but know that you may die before this is over."

"No," I said. I felt stronger than I ever had before, when I looked around me and saw the creatures in the woods—unicorns and griffins and small two-legged dragons and a laughing goat. And the fox who was a cat who was Jonah.

They belonged to my brother, and they were worth saving, no matter what the cost.

We were close to the edge of the cliff then, and ahead of us, several people—Mudwalkers!—hurried along, touching their torches to the dry brush and lowest branches of the trees. Fire licked up the trees and someone laughed. Mrs. Fletcher!

I did not stop to think, but rushed ahead, straight

toward her, screaming at the top of my voice. They hesitated, seeming surprised, and turned away, to face the edge of the cliff as if they might try to descend to the beach below.

But one did not. Mr. Blade, whose face was an animal's and whose body was twisted and ugly. He pushed past them, straight for me.

The fox leaped for his throat and was thrown aside. The great dragon's jaws opened menacingly, and Blade thrust his torch into its mouth. Still he came on, fire following him like a curse.

Will was beside me then. "If we can capture him and keep him until he can't hold his Mudwalker shape, he'll be as vulnerable as I am. He'll need trees, too, but he'll have a refuge where there are no creatures left. We can't let him escape to it."

We fell on Blade, many of us, bodies tangling and jaws savaging. Together we pulled him over the cliff, and we fell with him, landing on the rocks. I never let go of his arm, in spite of the pain that shot through my ribs. The Wyvern thrashing beside me shifted his jaws closer to my hands, bore down on Blade's arm, and grunted with satisfaction as bone crunched and Blade groaned. The Chimera shape-shifted from beast to man to beast, but we held him down, the creatures and I, until he was exhausted. And then the dragon and the winged serpent dragged him toward the water. But he began to struggle again, and I understood why. They were going into the water with him, and they would hold him down, away from the forest, for as long as it took for him to die. Even if they might die with him.

He screamed, and the fire behind us rose higher. Somewhere I could hear the Fletchers laughing.

My brother, knee deep in water, turned to look back at me. "Go before you're hurt," he said.

"No!" I shouted, and I ran down the beach, to be whatever help I could. The fox panted beside me, warning me about the fire.

I stopped and looked behind. The woods closest to the cliff were flaming.

"Your brother must send the dragon back," the fox said. "He can call up a storm and fight the fire."

"But the Chimera will escape!" I said.

"Then we must hold him down," the fox said. He shape-shifted awkwardly, as if it had become almost too difficult for him. "I will help you keep the Chimera from the forest for as long as I can."

We changed places with the dragon, who roared back toward Darkwood. Thunder and lightning broke over us and rain pelted us. Jonah and I and the winged serpent pulled the Chimera into the water so far that Jonah and I could only keep afloat by hanging on to the serpent. Every time the Chimera struggled to the top, we pushed him down. When the serpent and Jonah weakened, their places were taken by a griffin and a phoenix, and when they weakened, other creatures swam out to continue to battle. I shook with cold and half strangled on the salt water, but I would not let go of Blade's arm.

And then I saw the seal woman, the Kelpie, walking across the water that fell still before her in a shimmering path, and orcas swam beside her, rolling in the surf as if they were playing. And filled with confidence.

She walked close to me and said, "Let go, Charlotte. They won't mean to hurt you, but they might."

I let go of Blade and the orcas jerked him away, dragging him farther out into the Sound—into the dark—and the Kelpie walked beside them, her long hair streaming in the wind, her arms upraised. And then I could see nothing more.

I was close to drowning. The winged serpent was exhausted, too, gasping beside me, but she grabbed my shirt and pulled me to shore. I lay on the rocks for a long time, too tired to raise my head. I could smell smoke and hear, somewhere, shouts and screams.

Then, long after, the storm blew away to the north and the sky cleared. Stars looked down on me in the silence.

"Get up," the unicorn colt said. "My mother said you have to get up." She butted me painfully in the ribs and I sat up.

The fire was out.

"How many were hurt?" I asked, my voice shaking. "Is my brother still alive?"

"He is resting in the Wyverns' den. My mother says you must come."

She tried to pull me up the sandy cliff but she was not strong enough. I was trapped halfway to the top by my own weakness, until the serpent came and dragged me the rest of the way. The fire in the woods closest to us was out, but the air smelled of acrid smoke. "Is everyone alive?" I asked the Midwife.

"Alive—and grateful to you for nearly giving your life for us," she said. "But the Guardians are waiting for you, and your sister and other Mudwalkers are screeching out on the road. Do something to shut them up and make them go away. We can't have so much attention drawn to us. Who knows what one of them might see?"

"I have to take my brother back," I said.

Her head rose above me and I saw her fangs. "No. We are grateful, but we are not fools."

"I must take him back," I said. "He is still my parents' child."

Her head sank down to the level of mine. "Ah. *That.*"

"Yes, that," I said. "I'm going to take him back to Gull Walk with me. And we will decide later what we can do." I was exhausted and beginning to be aware that my left arm had been burned. I did not have the strength to argue with a creature so huge and dangerous, but I was determined to have my own way. "We will decide later!" I cried. "Will comes with me!"

I shouted his name until he came, so changed that I could barely recognize him. His skin was silver, like his hair, and he was taller and even thinner. The creatures called him a Fair One? Yes, he was fair, so beautiful that seeing him hurt my eyes.

"Will, come back with me," I said. "Think of our parents—Mama in the hospital and Dad so far away. How can they lose you?"

"How can Darkwood lose me?" he asked.

"Oh, Will, please!" I begged. "As long as you're at Gull Walk, you can come and go the way Jonah does."

"The way Jonah does," a dozen voices echoed. "Yes, he could do that."

"Until you're grown," I told Will. "When you're grown, then you could stay." That would be years in the future, I thought. Who could tell what might happen before then? There was no way of knowing what lay between that moment and the time when Will might rule Darkwood, as he should.

I reached out my hand to him and he took it. We walked out of the woods together, to greet Meg, the women who had been staying at Gull Walk, and dozens of people from town who had been drawn by the fire.

"I thought you were both dead!" Meg screamed. "Why did you do it? Why did you go into the woods?"

"We went after Jonah," the Warders said. "Charlotte and Will shouldn't have followed us, but everyone is all right now. The fire is out and the woods are safe."

They took us away, hurrying us down the road toward Gull Walk, before anyone could ask us questions. Will was only Will now, a frail boy who looked ready to cry, and Jonah, shuffling along behind us and scowling, was only exasperating Jonah, barefoot and grubbier than ever.

The night was over.

The Fletchers apparently left Gull Walk in their car that night—without paying their bill, of course. One of the three women staying there was a nurse, and she dressed the burn on my arm. It was not a large burn, and it had the curious shape of a unicorn's head, almost like a brand. But only Jonah remarked on it, rudely, of course.

Meg moved back to Seattle to stay with her best friend, and the Warders contacted my father, asking that Will and I be allowed to stay with them during the next school term, since we were happy there.

Sometimes the creatures asked my brother to bring me to the woods, and believing but not believing, I would sit by the pond with a unicorn baby napping beside me and watch the Spirit Lights dance.

And so the summer ended.

Afterward

Charlotte Thacker's father did not return to the country until the end of World War II. Her mother died in the sanatorium shortly afterward. Charlotte lived at Gull Walk with Will and the Warders until she went away to college.

In 1980, she left the country to study a rain forest in South America, the last of many such journeys. White deer—or small white horses—had been reported in the area. She was seen by an American couple at an open-air market, buying food, in the company of a boy. Later, Belgian tourists reported watching a woman of her description walk into the forest with a dog that resembled a fox. She never came out.

The strange white animals were seen occasionally in the distance until 1985, when the forest was burned down by farmers to make room for crops. Within three years, the shallow soil was exhausted, crops failed, and the farmers moved on.

JEAN THESMAN has written several award-winning novels for teenagers. She is a member of both the Authors Guild and the Society for Children's Book Writers and Illustrators (SCBWI). She lives in Washington State.